THE TERMS

Ruby Rowe

Contents

NOTES

The Terms: Part One is told from the points of view of
Camilla and Ellis.

This novel ends in a cliffhanger. It contains explicit language
and graphic sex, including aspects of BDSM.

DEDICATION

To the love of my life, Patrick.

CHAPTER ONE

Camilla

"Only you could be this attractive after death," I mumble, "and maybe that evil brother of yours." Damn, is it wrong I'm admiring a man who's lying in a casket? Dead at thirty-three. That's crazy, and what happened for you to die so young?

I need to wrap this up before I'm noticed. Surely, those three cars in the parking lot belong to the funeral staff. I mean, there's only five minutes left of visitation and a foot of snow on the ground.

After glancing around to ensure I'm alone in the room, I reach in my purse and retrieve the small photo of my little one. Eyeing his cute chubby cheeks, I then tuck the picture beneath Tony's arm that's resting peacefully over his stomach.

That sweet boy is the innocence, love and hope to all the dark perversion I witness every night at my job. There is not a greater gift than the love he gives back to me.

"Maybe I should've told you Liam was your son," I mutter, "but what if you'd taken him from me? I understand he needs a father, too, but he deserves one who isn't into shady–dangerous–shit. You asshole.

"Why did you have to make me the pawn in your twisted plan? I'd be grateful you're in this casket if it weren't for Liam. He was the payoff for my deceit, not your dirty money; however, now I'm left with this guilt.

3

"After how you treated me, I shouldn't feel guilty that you missed out on the opportunity to meet him, but I do, and it's only because he's so special.

"Maybe you would've provided for him and left us alone ... or maybe you would've used your power and wealth to take him from me. I couldn't risk it.

"If you can hear me right now, I pray you understand the tangled web you placed me in. You left me no other choice."

"Excuse me, Ms.," a male voice says from behind me. I hesitate before turning around and surveying the short, older male with a warm smile.

The words *funeral director* are etched on the gold name tag over his maroon suit jacket, so I sigh with relief. "I'm sorry, dear, but I must close up. You're welcome to return in the morning before the service begins."

"I apologize for keeping you here. I'm leaving now." Without waiting for a response, I hurry from the room. Once I reach the lobby, my heels echo the sound of a tap dance on the marble floor of the quiet space. Ten more feet, and I'll be out of this depressing joint.

"Wait," a different male voice demands.

Fight, flight, or freeze...

God, why did I freeze?

Inhaling sharply, I pivot to face him. The man is now standing in close proximity, his narrowing gaze studying me while the memories of the night I met him pepper my mind.

"How do you know my brother?"

Ellis Burke ... still ruggedly handsome to the point of unnerving. Tall and intimidating, causing my gaze to falter.

"Hello. I, uh, briefly dated Tony several years ago. I only wanted a moment to say goodbye, and now I'm leaving." I begin to turn, but he grabs my arm.

"That's why you look familiar, but I can't place where we met. I'm Ellis Burke." Easing free from his hold, I stare at the red tie beneath his distinguished grey suit.

"We've never met before, so I must resemble someone else. I should be going. The roads will be freezing soon."

"What is your name?" His voice reverts to its original demanding tone.

"It's Camilla Rose." *I'm so stupid. I should've given him another name. Better yet, I should've taken my friend Christopher's advice and not come here.*

"Are you OK? You seem nervous." He's on to me, and I can't have that, so I lift my chin and brave a look at him.

His striking eyes, a velvet blue, squint in confusion as he scrolls through the files of memories in his mind, searching for the one with my name on it. I've prayed to God every day for several years that he never remembers.

"I'm not nervous. I'm–I'm in mourning and worried about the weather."

"Then allow me to give you a ride home." Still scrutinizing me, he slides his fingers through the top of his light brown hair, pushing it back.

"I would prefer to drive. It was nice meeting you, Mr. Burke." I can't shove through the glass doors fast enough, and

5

once my heels hit the mixture of salt and ice on the concrete, I do an embarrassing jig to regain my footing. Thankfully, I'm blessed with great balance and coordination from all my years of dance.

I recall the dream I had as a child of becoming a professional ballerina. That aspiration was squelched for numerous reasons, but I have other dreams, and I'll make them come true for Liam. By the time he's a young man, he'll be proud of his mother.

CHAPTER TWO

Two Weeks Later

Camilla

"Thank you for watching him here. I know your parents prefer that you babysit at my apartment, but my sister relapsed in her recovery again, and she needs a place to stay."

Squatting down, I remove Liam's scarf and coat. "I have to limit his exposure to Sasha when she's like this." He yawns, and I attempt to flatten his brown hair that's woven with auburn strands. It has succumbed to static, leaving my kiddo looking like a miniature Einstein.

I admire how his *Batman* pajamas hug his little body in the cutest way. He hasn't lost his toddler belly yet, which makes him all that more adorable.

"My parents are going to bed soon, so they don't mind." After reaching back to tighten her blond ponytail, Hailey picks Liam up and cuddles him close to her. He rests his head on her shoulder, and I wish I could stay home with him tonight so he could cuddle with me instead.

"Do you want to watch your *Ninja Turtles* movie before bedtime?" she asks. I laugh when his head shoots up and he claps.

"We watch it now," he says.

"Sure, and since you're wide awake, maybe this time you'll make it through a whole thirty minutes of the movie before falling asleep."

Hailey giggles, and I hate thinking about how she's almost finished with college and will be pursuing her career. It's going to be difficult to find a sitter who measures up to her.

***

In the parking lot of Octavia, Denver's swankiest gentlemen's club, I turn off the ignition of my car and hunch over. Every aspect of the sleek black building's architecture is alluring for the affluent and dominating males.

The word *Octavia* is above the front glass doors in silver, and just beneath the roof, small blue bulbs line the perimeter of the building.

That's it. Simple. Streamlined. Classy. Yet every time I enter or exit this fine establishment, I feel dirty, and it's because I still have the memories of what I *used* to do here.

Every male who I've ever encountered inside has been polite, but they don't give a damn about my brains or heart. They want to use me, along with every other attractive employee, to satisfy their carnal appetite.

I found that out the hard way when I met Tony, except he wanted to use my sex appeal for something more complex and dangerous.

I can't stall the inevitable any longer, so I lock up my car and walk toward the employee entrance at the side of the building.

"Camilla, my cannoli girl. How are you this lovely evening?" Bruce asks after opening the door for me. Even the security guys in the back of the club wear suits, and his is becoming tight around his belly. "I saw that," he adds with a brow cocked.

"Saw what?"

"I watched you looking at my gut." He rubs a hand over his stomach. "It's your damn fault."

Planting a hand on my hip, I tilt my head to the side.

"Oh, I have to hear this."

"You bring me one of your homemade desserts twice a week. Times that by fifty-two weeks, and you get at least twenty extra pounds. Damn, girl. Times that by how many years?"

I can't help but snicker. "OK, I take full responsibility. No more desserts."

"Whoa, whoa, now. I didn't say anything about cutting me off. I just don't want you poking fun of my belly."

"Aww, I'm only playin'. There's more of you for the ladies to love on, and there's nothing wrong with that."

"There you go." His head nods in agreement. "We're on the same page now." Before I start toward the ladies' dressing room, we high-five, and his hand sails over his dark curls.

I stride down the dimly lit hallway, and once I reach my locker, I swap out my jeans and boots for my sequin silver skirt and black strappy heels.

As soon as I stand in the uncomfortable shoes, I think about Liam again and imagine being in my pajamas, sleeping next to him in our bed. I miss the sweet kid already. Sighing, I lock up my belongings and walk over to a mirror.

"Have at it, sweetheart," Gracie says, holding out her makeup brush that's been dipped in a shimmery powder. She's sitting next to me, primping before her shift as a dancer.

I swipe the brush over my chest and dust off the extra that has landed on my tight black top. We have a routine, Gracie and I do, and she's the only person in this club who I will see outside of it.

Remembering I need to get my girls out, I push them up from my bra until cleavage is spilling over it. Lastly, I tease my long auburn hair at the scalp to appear sexier, and that's about as good as it gets.

"Thank you. I'm off to serve drinks."

"Oh, I almost forgot... Matt wants to see you in his office before you hit the bar."

"Hmm ... OK." Striding down the hallway, I come to my boss's door and tap on it.

"Come in."

"Hi. Gracie said you wanted to see me?"

His eyes only glance up as he hands me a paper.

"First thing in the morning, go to this lab, and take a random drug test."

"Since when do you order *random* drug tests?"

"I knew you weren't going to make this easy," he mumbles before he sits back in his chair and looks at me. "Someone called and reported that you're on drugs, so I have to check."

"Seriously? Matt, you know how I feel about drug use. I even confided in you about Sasha's addiction."

"Sorry, but Marianne took the call. You know she's a snitch and will tell James if I don't investigate. What's the big deal? Go take it, you'll pass, and then we can move on from whatever drama you're obviously involved in."

Having a younger, arrogant boss is annoying. I just want to mess up that stiffly-styled, preppy hair of his.

"The big deal is that someone did this to me, and I have no clue who it was."

"They wouldn't give a name, and I don't care. Just take the damn test."

***

Pulling my wool coat tighter, I cross the parking lot after my shift. At 2:00 a.m., it's even colder than when I arrived. I love the scenery of Denver, but I'm over the Colorado winters and miss the warmth of South Carolina where I grew up.

I can see my breath as I curse over how early I have to be at the lab for the drug screen. Add in the anger brewing over the three men who managed to cop a feel tonight, and I'm in a peach of a mood. Picking up my pace, I reach my car and shove my key in the lock.

"Clarissa Rosenthal."

My real name ... and that voice.

"Now that I have your attention, turn around," he says.

Gradually, I shift to face him. Ellis Burke is in the backseat of a black Mercedes sedan with the window lowered. The others are tinted, so I can't make out who's driving.

"I know you're a hacker by trade, but I can't fathom how you uncovered my real name."

"We need to have a discussion. Get in."

"I'm not getting inside your car. I'm tired and have to get a ridiculous drug test in only five hours."

"And if you want to pass that test, you'll get in my car this instant." A smug smile eases from his lips.

"You made the call to Octavia, but why?"

He holds up the photo I'd placed in Tony's casket. Seeing my son's smile leaves me gasping for breath.

"Get in the car, Camilla, if you don't wish to lose your child."

With the mention of Liam, I march to his window.

"Don't you threaten me, and don't you dare mention my son. Don't even think about him, and give me that damn photograph."

His smirk vanishes. "I'm not a man you want to cross. Get. In. This. Car."

"Fine. You have five minutes to explain what this is about." Crossing my arms, I stomp around to the passenger side, and a driver exits the vehicle. Expressionless, he opens the door for me.

Be stoic, Camilla.

I tell myself that, but I'm screwed. Somehow, Ellis knows too much already. I get in the backseat, and as I sink against the leather beneath me, I inhale its scent of wealth and power. "How did you discover my identity?"

"Hacking has made me a great detective."

"What do you want? And can I have my picture back?"

"Did you, or did you not, withhold from Tony that he had a son?" He holds a hand up. "And I caution you to answer honestly. I have ways of knowing everything."

"I never should've gone to the funeral home." My head falls back against the seat. "I only went out of guilt. I imagine like Tony, you have no idea what that emotion feels like."

"Answer the question, Camilla, or would you prefer I call you Clarissa?"

"Don't ever say that name again, and yes, I withheld the information from Tony." Rolling my head in his direction, I prepare to face his anger.

His fingers tug on his full lower lip as he examines the photograph, so I study him while I wait. Instead of a suit tonight, he's in khakis and a navy sport coat over a pale blue shirt.

"That's what I suspected. This kid looks just like a Burke."

I swipe the photo from his hand. "I obviously had good reason to hide it from him. Both of you are heartless. Now, what do you want?"

"Your son is going to be raised as a Burke."

"Ha! Fat chance of that happening. I don't want him anywhere near your diabolical family."

My chin is clenched by his strong fingers. He turns my head toward him and leans in. Even in the dim light, his eyes are vivid, alluring like the rest of him, and I'm pissed with myself for finding him attractive.

My gaze shifts to the partition, and I wish the driver could hear and see this, but would he even help me?

"Listen to me. On account of your deceit, and the circumstances you've created, I have terms you're going to follow. If you don't agree to those terms, then I *will* take your son away. It would be easy to do once a judge heard the details of your sordid life.

"First, you'll have failed your drug test, which I can have happen with a few keystrokes. On top of that, you're a washed-up dancer turned bartender, have a strung-out sister crashing in your atrocious apartment, and well, I don't have to explain to you the shit I could cause with a phone call to your parents.

"I can see it in the papers now. 'Many years later, the mystery is solved as to the disappearance of Clarissa Rosenthal and her sister, Sasha.'" Holding his hands up, he spreads them out. "The word 'kidnapping' would be in bold as the headline."

Tears well up in my eyes, and my lower lip quivers.

"Tony was right; you're evil."

His fingers grip my chin and press harder this time.

"I knew he'd cause me grief from the grave. You and *Tony Jr.* are interruptions I don't need, but my parents deserve to know their only grandchild.

"For that reason, I'll allow this situation to disrupt my world. Besides, it will be good to have another male to carry on the family name."

"Please, leave us be. Let me raise Liam. I promise I'm a good mother. I struggle financially, but he's always cared for and loved."

Desperation tips the scale, and my lukewarm tears tumble to my cool cheeks. Looking away, Ellis clears his throat and releases my chin.

"Money, right... I recommend you change the password to your bank account to something more challenging. It was quite easy to empty that miniscule nest egg of yours."

From my dry throat, a sob emerges. He's going to take Liam away and leave me homeless. I have no choice but to play by his rules, so I cough from my cry and suck in short breaths, attempting to collect my dignity. Sniffling, I pull a tissue from my purse and wipe my eyes.

"OK, I'll do whatever you want. Please, please, don't take my child from me."

Snaking his fingers through my hair, his thumb skims along my cheekbone, wiping away the tears. He moves closer, his sultry breath inches from mine, and his eyes roam my face as if he's admiring a gallery painting.

"There's no need to cry. If you're open to this, your life will be easier—better even. Do exactly as I say, and you won't lose Liam."

I should shove him away. Spit in his face. Anything other than what I'm doing, which is leaning into his hand at my cheek to savor his touch.

I'm emotionally fucked in the head, always finding myself attracted to the villain instead of someone nice, like my friend Christopher, for instance.

As if Ellis feels something, too, he withdraws his hand.

"First, you're going to quit your job."

"What? That's crazy. I have to work."

"Liam is a Burke. His mother is not going to be employed at a strip club. Instead, you can finish earning that worthless degree you've been working toward for years."

"There's nothing worthless about public service."

An eye roll confirms his smugness. "Then, in two weeks, you'll move into my home. It's over 15,000 square feet, so there's plenty of room. You'll like it. It's much nicer than that *dwelling* you're in now."

"I can't live with you. I don't even know you, Liam will be scared, and I can't give up my place. My sister has nowhere else to go."

"Do as I say, and I'll return your money. You can use it to keep your apartment."

"If I'm not working, I'll burn through that money in no time."

"We'll cross that bridge when the time comes. I'm also hiring a nanny to help with Liam's care. He'll have a tutor, as well."

"A tutor? He's three, Ellis, and I have an amazing sitter. Liam adores her." My chin is grasped once more but gently this time. His thumb grazes across my bottom lip as he eyes it intently.

"Although it's pointless for you to challenge me, I'm surprised by how much I like your attempts. I also enjoy hearing my name from these pouty red lips."

I swallow, my throat further parched from the burning gaze I feel on me. "There are more terms you must agree to, an *intimate* one in particular, but we'll save that conversation for a later date."

What the hell? Does he think I'm going to be some kind of sex slave?

"Don't touch me." Jerking free, I huff and fling my head back against the seat. "I can't believe this is happening."

"You caused this. My brother had many less-than-desirable traits, but regardless, he deserved to be a part of his child's life. Maybe he'd be alive today had he known of Liam's existence."

I cross my arms and glare at him. "Tony hated you."

"Your words can't hurt me. I don't feel things the way other people do."

"That's evident."

"Get out of my car. A moving company will be arriving in two weeks to pack up your things. In the meantime, I advise that you separate what you'd like to keep with you, seeing as how the rest is going into storage."

Shoving the door open, I step out. "Oh, and, Ms. Rose, since we both know you're a runner, it's important I state that you better stay put. If not, I *will* find you and remove Liam from your custody. With the luxury of a laptop, I can give you any identity I choose. You've been warned."

"For the record, I hate you, too!" Slamming the door, I stand in the cold air and cry. The car drives away, and my head hangs in defeat. There is no way out for my sweet child and me. I'll never forgive myself for getting involved with Tony Burke.

CHAPTER THREE

Camilla

Through my nose, I suck in a breath to stop it from running. Tears are still falling to my coat, and I'm trembling as I approach my ground-floor apartment.

The rock music playing inside can be heard at the door, so I assume Sasha is still up. I step inside and *oh, hell no*. A guy I've never seen before is in my recliner, and a jerk Sasha used to date is cozy next to her on the couch. The place reeks of weed, too.

"Out! Out of my apartment now." The unfamiliar male stands and looks to me, but Rusty and Sasha don't seem to have a care in the world.

She shrugs. "Her house, her rules." She can hardly hold her eyelids open, and I picture myself throwing a glass of water in her face. I'm furious.

Rusty gives her a disgusting, sloppy kiss, and as he and the strange guy approach me, he grimaces.

"We're back together, so you better get used to me being around."

"Says the loser who's standing in the apartment *I* pay for. Don't show your face here again."

"Sis!" Sasha yells.

"You better watch it, lady. You *do not* want to piss me off," he threatens before going out the door. Once I've slammed it shut, I remove my coat and boots and turn off the old stereo sitting on my small entertainment center.

"Did you hear him? Are you trying to get us hurt?"

Her hand waves toward me. "He doesn't mean it."

"I was adamant that you were to have no one in this apartment. I also made it crystal clear that you were never to bring drugs here or get back with Rusty."

Scowling, she tucks her caramel-colored hair behind her ear. "It's only pot, and you can't stop me from dating someone."

"Your behavior could cause me to lose Liam. You can't begin to comprehend the weight of stress on me to keep us safe and afloat." The next thing I know, I'm sobbing again. Plopping down on my couch, I bury my face in my hands.

"Damn, sis. What happened to you?" I feel the cushions sink in as she moves closer. She rubs my back, and I wish that after all the support I've shown her over the years, she could save me from this nightmare, but I know better. Falling back, I stare up at the ceiling.

"You know how I told you Liam's father died?"

"Yeah."

"I did a stupid, stupid thing. I went to the funeral home to put a photo of Liam in his casket. His brother saw me and did his research. He knows who I really am—who you are, and he's blackmailing me."

"Oh, shit. What does he want?"

"He's demanding that Liam be raised in his home, and he wants me to live there, too. I don't know all the details, but he's forcing me to quit my job and move in with him."

"Where the hell will I go?"

Turning my head, I glare at her. "That would be your first thought."

"I'm sorry," she utters. Her gaze shifts to the carpet, and she bites her lip.

"I'm going to use my savings to pay for the apartment. You can stay here, but not for long, Sasha. Three months tops, and I mean it this time. You have to get it together, work and find a place of your own. You're twenty-five and don't have a damn thing to show for it."

"OK, OK. I get what a disappointment I am. I'll figure something out." Like always, Sasha jumps to her feet to put an end to our conversation.

If she had a room of her own, she'd march there to escape, but since this apartment is small, she has to crash on the couch. Instead, she stomps to the kitchenette right off the living room and opens the fridge. As I examine her, I shake my head.

It's early February, yet for some reason, she's in a snug white tank top. Once she leans over to grab a soda, the ladybug tattoo above her ass is visible. She's too skinny, yet her jeans are way too tight, and her shoulder-length hair is tangled and dirty. My sister looks trashy, and I hate it.

I wanted so much more for her. Hell, I fought and risked everything so she could have more, but I'm finding the damage is irreversible. I fear her emotional scarring will never heal. Turning to face me, she hugs her hip.

"Are you going to bed soon? I'm really tired."

"Sure, Sasha. I'll get out of your way," I reply sarcastically.

"God, I'm sorry, OK? I'm just tired."

"So am I, and unlike you, I only get to sleep for a few hours before I have to get up again."

"What are you going to do about that guy, Liam's uncle?" Her eyes widen. "Wait, does he know about what happened to him?"

"No, and you're never to speak of it. If he shows up here, you know nothing." Hopping up, I march to her and grip her shoulders.

"Promise me, Sasha. Promise me, because if Ellis Burke finds out what his brother made me do to him, he'll take Liam for good. He might even hurt us."

"I promise I won't say anything. I'd never put you or Liam in danger."

"Good, and Christopher can't hear of the truth, either." Feeling a headache coming on, I rub my forehead. "I dread breaking the news to him about Ellis. What excuse could I possibly give him?"

I exhale, but not an ounce of weight is lifted from my chest. I've come unglued tonight, and it has to stop here, or I'll lose Liam. I'm putting back on my armor. I'll do what Ellis commands and be whoever he desires if it keeps me with my son.

Ellis

"Come in," I say after the tap on my office door.

"Here's your cup of coffee, Mr. Burke," Irene says in her Italian accent. Her head is down as she scurries to my desk. "I hope it's just the way you like it."

She's out as fast as she came in, and it's probably because I was a dick to her this morning before the first cup. As I pick up the mug, I wave my hand toward Christopher, my new assistant.

"Do something for her. Maybe give her a half day off Friday with pay, and be prepared to do more groveling gestures on my behalf. I tend to take my frustrations out on my staff."

"Yes, sir." He smirks, and now he's the dick. "Rough night?" he adds.

"I had some personal business to handle, but due to the nature of it, I have to fill you in on some of the details." Getting comfortable in the wingback chair to the right of my desk, he takes a drink from his travel mug. "A woman and her child are moving in with me."

Aaaand, he spits out the drink from his travel mug. His eyebrows are raised high as he grabs tissues from a box on my desk and begins cleaning the iPad in his lap. I think coffee even landed in his black hair.

"Sorry, *sir*, but can you repeat that? I'm sure I heard you wrong." He pats at his now stained dress shirt.

I roll my eyes. "OK, you got your *sirs* in. Now, stop being an ass. You know what I said."

"You really are irritable this morning."

"Just because you're working for me now, instead of Tony, doesn't mean you need to call me sir."

"I was only joking, but in all seriousness, what's this about a woman and child?"

"You know that non-disclosure agreement you signed?"

"Of course."

"Remember again that you signed it. This information doesn't leave your lips, or I'll sue your ass." Leaning back, I thread my fingers behind my head. "Tony has a three-year-old son, and that child and his mother are moving in here. I will be supporting them."

Coughing repeatedly, he smacks his chest.

"I know it's surprising. Are you OK?"

"Yeah, uh, wow. Tony had a kid?"

"Yes, and he didn't know it. Wait, you were the closest person to him. He had no clue, right?"

"Of course not."

"Her name is Camilla Rose. Do you recall ever meeting her or hearing Tony mention her name?"

His eyes flit to the door as he thinks.

"No, I can't recall the name. So, did you approach her, or did she contact you?"

I give him a pointed look.

"I'm a private person, Christopher. Maybe you were used to asking Tony questions about his business, but I don't operate that way. I'll only be sharing details about my life if they're relevant to the matters you're handling."

Nodding, he glances to his iPad. "I understand."

"Good. You couldn't have come on board at a better time, so get ready to take notes. We have a lot to accomplish before they arrive."

CHAPTER FOUR

Camilla

"Cammy, get up. Christopher's here and needs to talk to you," Sasha says from the other side of my bedroom door.

I sit up, and it startles Liam, so he wakes from his nap, too. Of course, this is the only time I can ever get any sleep. Why didn't Chris just text me?

Climbing out of bed, I mess with my hair, straightening it the best I can. I'm only in sweats and an oversized t-shirt. "Camilla," Sasha says after cracking open my door.

"I heard you. Give me a minute."

"Momma," Liam says in his whiny voice as he holds his arms up for me to take him. I scoop him up, and before I head out to the living room, I dig for a mint in my purse and pop it in my mouth.

"Chris is here to see us," I say in an excited tone. Grinning, my kiddo rubs sleep from his eye with his fist. We stroll into the family room, and I spot Christopher in the recliner. While tapping his foot, he stares out my window.

"Hi, is everything all right? I wasn't expecting you."

He turns to me, and in an instant I suspect something's wrong. He's pale, and a look of anguish is owning his face.

"Chris," Liam says, reaching for our friend.

"Hey, buddy," he replies with only a faint smile. Straightening my hair some more, I study him. Even though he appears to have not slept, he's still dressed nice in slacks and an expensive button-up shirt.

"I'll be in your room if you need me," Sasha says. I nod before I direct my attention back to Chris.

"Come on, say something already."

Getting up, he strides over and wraps his arms around me, squishing Liam between us. He's hugged me in the past, but this is a different embrace. There's a desperation to it. Liam fusses, so Chris releases us.

Taking a seat on the couch, I slide my fingers through my little one's silky hair to calm him. He's clingy now, like he senses our friend isn't himself.

"I have to confess something to you, and I don't know what will happen after, so I want to tell you first how much you and Liam mean to me.

"You've become my world the last few years. I was by your side after he was born, and I've watched him grow. I feel like I've been a good friend to you."

My head shakes in confusion. "You have been. I don't understand what you're trying to say."

Pacing in front of me, he drags his hands down his face.

"I want more with you, Camilla. Have you ever thought about us being a couple? I could be a dad to Liam and take care of you. We could have a great life together." Dropping to his knees in front of me, he cups my face. "I want to be with you."

Am I still asleep and having a bad dream?

Pulling away, I stand and shove around him to walk to the kitchen. Without a word, I remove a sippy cup from the cabinet and fill it with milk before I take Liam to my bedroom where Sasha has already made herself at home.

"Sis, I need you to entertain Liam while I talk to Christopher. He probably needs to go to the bathroom, too." Without giving her a choice, I sit him on the bed next to her.

Ugh, I feel a pain in my lower back as I rise. He's getting too big for me to tote around. Returning to the living room, I blow out a breath.

"Have you lost your mind?" I ask. Christopher sits again in the recliner and rubs his forehead. "I don't know what happened to cause this desperation, but we're getting to the bottom of it. I have enough shit going on in my life, so this can't be another dark cloud hanging over my head."

"Just answer me, Cammy. Have you ever thought about me in that way?"

"No. We're only friends."

"Friends often turn into lovers."

"God, don't say that word. See, it's just—no." Shaking my head, I sit back down. "You're amazing, Chris, and attractive, but I don't have romantic feelings for you, and why in the world are you telling me this now?"

Releasing a yell of frustration, he grabs his hair, and I about come off of my couch from the shock of it. "What's happening? You're not yourself, and it's scaring me. Maybe you should go."

Looking to the window again, he exhales a long breath.

"I see there's no way around this conversation. If you wanted me like I've wanted you, we could move away from here, and I wouldn't have to confess this." Bringing his gaze back to me, he stares hard with his green eyes. "Tell me how you came in contact with Ellis Burke."

"What? How did you find out about that?"

"I know him."

"How?"

"I work for him."

"Once again, I don't understand. Explain."

Looking to the ceiling, his mouth moves, and is he for real saying a prayer right now? I'm about to kick his ass. "Tell me, Christopher, before I find a peanut and shove that allergen in your damn mouth."

"Damn, that's harsh. You'd kill me over this?"

"Seriously, if you're any kind of friend to me, you will tell me what the fuck's going on."

"I was Tony Burke's personal assistant for years, and once he discovered you were pregnant, he had me befriend you to find out what you were going to do about the baby."

Stunned, I stare at him. "After you had Liam and I gave Tony all the information he wanted, I never told him we stayed in contact."

"You were the friend I thought would never let me down," I whisper. Wondering if I could ever look at Chris in the eyes again, I stare at the tan carpet instead.

"I've had strong feelings for you for a while now, but out of respect for Liam's father, I've always shoved them down and dated other women, hoping like hell I'd fall in love with someone else.

"After Tony died, I thought maybe you and I *could* have a life together. Ellis offered me a job as his assistant last week, and I couldn't resist the money, thinking I could use it to care for you and Liam, but then this morning he dropped this bomb on me."

"So, Tony's the friend you said died."

"Yes, and now I'm supposed to be here handling affairs for Ellis, but I've been a fucking mess, going out of my mind over how to handle this."

"Why would Tony have you spy on me?"

"He wanted to ensure you weren't planning to cause him trouble. He said you held information you could use against him, and he also worried you might come after his money for Liam."

"Wow, and I thought he was a worthless bastard before I knew this."

"How did Ellis find out about you?"

"Against your wishes, I went to the funeral home. He did some digging after and figured it out. Now, he's blackmailing me. If I want to keep Liam, I have to move into his house so he can see to it Tony's child is raised as a Burke."

Once again, Christopher is right at my feet and on his knees. His hands grab mine, but I pull them away.

"Camilla, I'm sorry for what I did. If you'll give me a chance, I'll prove to you that you can trust me again. You don't have to live with Ellis. He can't prove you're unfit, so his threats mean nothing."

"He *does* have leverage against me. He knows things about my past that could cause me to lose Liam, and do you honestly think I want anything to do with you after this?"

Hanging his head, he stands. "I understand why you're pissed at me, and I deserve it, but the friendship I gave you all these years was genuine. You need me right now, Cammy. If you agree to Ellis's terms, then you're going to want a friend while you're living under the same roof as him.

"He can be difficult and demanding, and he's seldom around children. I'm also suspicious that he has another motive since bringing you and Liam there is out of character for him."

"I've taken care of myself for years now. I can handle Ellis Burke."

"This is different, and you know it. You don't get to be the one in control, and that's going to kill you inside. Let me help you through this. If he pulls anything, like if he changes his mind about taking Liam from you, maybe I can diffuse the situation. I'll also work on getting you out of this deal."

Looking up at him from the couch, I glare.

"Now you're manipulating me just like Tony and Ellis did."

"I'm trying to make this right, OK? And he's going to get suspicious if I don't return with the answers he wants from you."

"Fine, I'll tell him what he wants to know, but it doesn't mean I won't rat you out. I haven't decided."

He pulls out his cell phone.

"I need to work out a date and time I can have the movers here. Ellis would like you to begin staying with him next Friday, so why don't we have your belongings moved on Thursday. I imagine you'll need your things until then."

A thought hits me, and I look around the apartment.

"You only need to send a small truck and one person. I'm leaving my furniture here for Sasha, so I'll only have Liam's and my personal belongings. I won't need to put anything in storage like he suggested."

Nodding, he types away on his phone.

"I'm supposed to tell him things that Liam likes."

"What do you mean?"

He looks off. "Like colors, toys ... things of that nature. It's for his bedroom."

"He doesn't need anything special. He's been sleeping with me up until this point, and I imagine that'll continue."

"Ellis insisted Liam have his own room, so I'll just tell him he likes superheroes, trucks and trains. Books... Oh, and how he absolutely loves *Ninja Turtles*." Christopher smiles, and it angers me.

He does know my son and has been good to him, but I don't want to forgive him for what he did. Although, maybe I should use his help like he suggested since he owes me that much.

"Ellis also asked for a list of foods you both enjoy. He wants to ensure the kitchen is fully stocked for the two of you, so I'll write that down for him, as well. I know what you and Liam like to eat."

I can't help but shake my head. This is too bizarre. Even if Ellis sincerely wishes to know his nephew, I can't comprehend why a handsome, wealthy, single man would move us into his home.

"OK, I'll accept your help," I say.

Glancing up from his phone, Chris's eyes display relief.

"Thank you. I'll feel better knowing I can watch out for you and Liam."

"I guess it would be nice to have a familiar face nearby while I'm stuck in that mansion with the *evil one*."

"Don't worry. We'll get through this together." Christopher stands and strolls to the door. "I think that's all we need to discuss for now."

"Wait, I have something for you to relay to Ellis," I say. "Tell him I insist on interviewing candidates for the nanny position. I deserve to be involved in that decision."

"I agree. I'll be in touch, and thank you for not shutting me out."

"This doesn't mean we're friends. I'm allowing your help because you owe me big time. Don't get the two confused."

Frowning, he disappears through the doorway, and good gracious, our lives have been turned upside down.

***

"You're quitting?" Matt asks. He's looking straight at me for a change.

"I know it's sudden. I can give you a week's notice, and you can deduct the cost of the drug screen from my last paycheck."

33

"Who hired you?"

"Um, actually, I met someone. He's going to provide me support while I finish my degree."

"I haven't heard a word about you being in a relationship. Have you been keeping it under wraps because it's a client?"

I sigh. He's the first of several people who will question me over this.

"No, he's not a client. I didn't meet him here. Look, you know I'm independent, so leaving Octavia is hard enough without me having to explain myself."

His brow knits. "All right. Whatever you need to do. Unlike the younger servers, who want to take a break every goddamn minute, you work hard. If you ever need to come back, you're welcome to."

I smile. "You mean as long as I don't age or gain twenty pounds, right?"

Motioning toward the door, he smirks.

"You're only twenty-nine; you have at least a few hot years left in you. Go to work before this gets sentimental. I have a reputation to uphold."

Repeatedly, I've prayed to get out of this demeaning place, but at least here, I know what to expect when I walk through the doors.

I'm in the dark over what Ellis Burke has planned for me behind his closed doors. If I read him right, my life won't be less demeaning anytime soon.

***

I'm exhausted and emotionally spent as I stride to the exit of Octavia. My only female friend here, Gracie, is now pissed at me. She thinks I've been hiding a relationship from her, and it's frustrating that I can't tell her the truth.

I could possibly confide in her, but since I'm not a hundred percent sure, protecting Liam and Sasha must come before protecting a friendship. It sucks.

Once I reach the exit, Bruce's mouth droops.

"I heard the news, my cannoli girl. It breaks my heart."

"I'm sorry, Bruce. I really am. Maybe I can bring you by a dessert once in a while." I smile, hoping he'll do the same to ease my guilt.

"That would be great. Then, I can be sure you're doing OK." He pulls out his wallet. "Here's my business card. You know I watch out for you ladies when you're walking through the parking lot late at night.

"Well, I saw you get in that luxury ride last night. I wasn't trying to be nosy; I was only concerned. Anyway, you were upset after, and now you're quitting. I can't help but wonder if the two are related."

"Bruce, I appreciate the concern, but I can't discu—"

"Stop right there," he exclaims with his hands up. "I don't expect you to tell me anything about last night. Just promise me if you're ever in trouble and need help, you'll call me at that number. I'll be by your side in a flash to assist any way I can."

35

My eyes wash with tears over his kindness. Maybe there are still people I can trust. Grabbing the big fella, I hug him hard.

"Thank you, Bruce."

CHAPTER FIVE

Ellis

After wiping the sweat from my brow, I scrub my face with my hands as if it will rub away the memory of the dream I just had. How could I forget it? It's always the same one.

The same blurred woman in red lingerie.

The same sensuous body pinned beneath mine.

The only feature I can make out is the unique color of her eyes, a hazel swirl of earthy green and brown.

What I can never sort out from my dream is why I'm so vulnerable when I'm physically on top of this woman. It's like I'm making love to her instead of fucking her hard, and that weakness is what drives me mad.

Why have I had these dreams for years? And why have they been more frequent since meeting Camilla Rose?

I tried dominating women in the bedroom once the dreams began, but it never helped. With Camilla, it will be different because it will be under duress ... at least in the beginning.

I'll see to it that she's the one who makes them stop. Her resistance is what I'm banking on to rid me of these nightmares. I'll be in control, her submission giving me peace.

Feeling hot under the silk sheet, I kick it off my body and expose my naked skin. The cool air calms me, and I sense sleep approaching, giving me a second chance for rest.

***

Hearing someone, I lift my eyes and find Christopher standing in my office doorway.

"Good morning," I say.

"Good morning. Camilla—I mean Ms. Rose and her son have arrived."

"OK, thank you." I return my attention to my laptop, but not sensing his departure, I look up again. "Is there something else?"

"I thought you'd want to come down to greet them."

"I told you to help them get settled in. I'll find them later."

"Of course."

God, what was I thinking? There's a three-year-old in my home this very instant, yet I don't know the first thing about relating to a toddler.

Second, his protective mother, who's accompanying him, is pissed at me and likely scared. I can't anticipate her moves just yet, so I'm having reservations about my decision to bring them here.

Third, I have Christopher to deal with. I only hired him because he was my brother's confidante. The circumstances surrounding Tony's death are being investigated, so I need to ensure he didn't leave additional messy loose ends, like another damn child.

After Christopher was evasive to my questions, I offered him a salary he couldn't refuse. I foresee him kissing my ass for a long time, during which I'll gain his trust and determine if anything is missing from the puzzle that makes up Tony Burke. My gut tells me my brother didn't take his own life.

Camilla

As I hold Liam close, his wide eyes scan the enormous room we're standing in. I'm not sure what to call it. It's too spacious to be considered a foyer. I'll call it the grand hall.

There's a sparkling chandelier above us that Liam points to, his back arching as he strains to stare at it in awe.

My back strains next as I try to pull him upright. We're waiting in front of a white floating staircase that Christopher ascended in order to speak to Ellis.

The way it curves above us is remarkable, but it's a total safety hazard for Liam. It's encased by a silver iron railing that I can picture him climbing.

My feet stand on a light grey marble floor you can almost see your reflection in from the sun's rays shining through a wall of windows. I know this because Liam has caught sight of his shadow and is now leaning over, hurting my back further.

"Kid, you're killing me," I whisper before I set his feet to the floor and take his hand. Seeing this as his green light to be rambunctious, he stomps on his shiny reflection with his tennis shoes, so to distract him, I squat and remove his hat and coat.

A grey-haired woman in a maid's uniform, similar to one you'd see worn in a hotel, scurries toward us.

"Oh, Ms., I'm so sorry. Mr. Day didn't tell me you arrived," she says with an Italian accent I recognize on the spot. It's comforting since my grandmother is Italian.

Nervously, she snatches Liam's outerwear from my hands, so I begin removing my coat. "I'm Mrs. Esposito, but Mr. Burke doesn't mind if you call me Irene," she announces.

"Hi, I'm Camilla Rose, and this is my son, Liam."

Irene leans over and shakes his little hand. This makes him feel big, so he grins at her, showing his white teeth, and I'm relieved he seems comfortable and excited in our new environment.

Hearing someone, I look up and watch Christopher as he walks down the steps alone.

"Would you like me to fix you some breakfast?" Irene asks.

"We've already eaten, but thank you."

"OK, but when you need anything at all, Ms. Rose, you ask me, and I'll be at your service."

"Thank you, and please call me Camilla."

"Ellis is working and will meet with you later," Christopher states as Irene strides away. "Let me show you around and get you settled in. You can spend today getting Liam comfortable in his new room and the rest of the house."

Pulling free from me, Liam runs to one of several stone columns that line the perimeter of the room. His short arms stretch around it, and he groans, thinking if he reaches enough, his fingers will touch on the opposite side. Not happening, kid.

"I guess he's going to like it here after all," Chris says in a sharp tone.

"Let's hope," I utter before I look at him. His eyes display sadness as he stares at Liam. He's not any happier about this

41

situation than I am, and things are awkward now that I know he desires me in a way I can't reciprocate.

"OK, let's get this over with." Walking over to Liam, I swoop him up into my arms and stroll back to Chris.

"You know, you'll have to stop carrying him soon."

"Not yet. I'm not ready. He's the only child I'll ever have, so I don't want to miss any of it." Realizing how personal my declaration is, I don't make eye contact. "Also, don't tell me how to parent. I already feel my control slipping away."

"I'm sorry." He points farther into the home. "Let's start this way."

Ellis

Standing outside of Liam's bedroom, I listen to Camilla speaking. Her voice is gentle as she reads him a book. At least, it sounds like she's reading.

"Momma, my room is big," he says.

"Geez, you really can't listen through a whole page, can you?" she asks. "Your room *is* big, and thank goodness there is a lot of room since you've dragged out every new toy.

"It's a mess in here. Hop up from my lap so we can clean this up before Mr. Burke comes in and we get in trouble."

"I'm in trouble, Momma?" he asks her, sounding concerned.

"No, sweetheart. Everything is fine. Just help me pick up."

This makes me scowl. She's truly afraid of me, and that's fine, but I don't want the kid scared of me, too. I need to get this over with, and the fact I'm nervous about it frustrates me.

Clearing my throat, I step into the doorway and find Camilla's shapely ass, snug in jeans, in my line of sight. She's bent over, picking up books.

"Good afternoon," I say. Whipping around, she loses her balance and falls backward, landing on a pile of toys. Oh, shit.

"Momma, you OK?" Liam asks her, his blue eyes round as they dart between the two of us. He squats next to her for protection and stares up at me.

Realizing I'm doing nothing, I scramble over to her and reach out my hand. She glowers at me before taking it, and her

43

body soon separates from an assortment of various shaped toys.

"I'm sorry. I didn't mean to startle you."

"It's fine." As soon as she's upright, she slides a hand across her lower back and rubs it.

"Are you hurt?"

"No, it's nothing." Her eyes are looking anywhere but at me.

"Did Chris give you a tour of the property?"

"Well, he tried, but we should've saved Liam's room for last. He hasn't wanted to leave it." Smiling, she finally tilts her hazel eyes up at me. "Thank you for all of this; however I do worry it could spoil him."

"Are you going to introduce me to my nephew?"

"OK, but we're saving the *uncle* talk with him for later"– leaning in close, her smile vanishes–"and don't get the wrong impression when I tell him we're friends. It's only to make him feel safe around you," she whispers.

Placing my fingers under her chin, I lift it up.

"Oh, Camilla, we're going to be *close* friends soon."

"We're not friends, and I'd slap your hand away if it wouldn't scare Liam. Don't ever touch me in front of him."

Dropping my hand, I grimace. "Introduce me so you and I can have a private discussion. We have some things to get straight."

Sighing, she turns back to Liam. He's staring up at us from the floor while playing with a truck in his hand.

"Liam, I want you to meet Mr. Burke."

"Ellis," I interject.

"We're going to call him Ellis. He's our new friend who bought you all these fun toys and made this nice bedroom for you."

His eyes never stray from mine as he stands and sidles up next to her leg. Wrapping his arm around it, he hugs it for dear life.

"Tell him thank you for the presents."

A faint smile curves from his lips as he gazes up at me and over my head like I'm the tallest man he's ever seen.

"Thank you for my toys."

"You're welcome. I can't get over how much he resembles the males in my family."

She ruffles Liam's hair with her hand.

"I wish he had inherited my hair or eye color, but no such luck for either one."

"I don't know. I see a touch of auburn in his light brown hair. He gets that from you." I pull my phone from my pocket. "I'm going to have Irene come up to watch him while we talk, but tomorrow we'll interview nannies and get someone hired right away."

"Wait." Her hand grabs my wrist, and her hot touch catches me off guard. I look down at her fingers wrapped tightly around my skin the way I'd like them to wrap around my cock.

Is it wrong I'm thinking about this in front of her kid? This is too confusing. Her hand releases me, so I meet her gaze. "I'm sorry, but could Mr. Day watch him? Liam took to him quickly."

For some reason, it irritates me that Liam is comfortable with Christopher already, but I'm going to have to bend a little for her to do the same.

"Fine." Hitting his number on my phone, I wait for him to answer.

"Christopher, please come to Liam's room—now."

CHAPTER SIX

Camilla

Giving a nervous smile at the doorway, Christopher strolls into Liam's room.

"Chris," Liam says, his eyes lighting up before he rushes past Ellis to show his old friend his new truck. *Shit!* I never thought of Liam outing us by way of his enthusiasm toward Christopher.

"Hi there, little buddy," Chris replies hesitantly. Ellis's furrowed brow doesn't go unnoticed.

"Well, it appears he likes you already," he scoffs. "Stay here and, uh, play with him while Camilla and I go discuss some things."

"Sure."

"Please watch that he doesn't run out of the room toward the staircase," I add.

Following Ellis to the door, my eyes round as I pass by Christopher. He's delivering the same nervous expression, and I imagine he's wondering, too, if we'll be able to pull this off.

"Have you seen your bedroom yet?" Ellis asks, not looking back at me.

"No. Like I said, we hit a roadblock once we reached Liam's room."

"Then we'll speak in there."

"Can't we talk elsewhere?"

"No," he quips.

Geez, he's annoying ... and sexy ... and moody it seems. Walking down the wide hallway, I try to pull my eyes away from his firm ass that's accentuated beneath a pair of black tailored dress pants.

He works from home, so I'm curious as to why he's wearing professional attire. Hell, I wouldn't get out of my pajama pants if I was working from home all day. Well, if it were just the three of us there: Liam, Sasha and me.

A panic over how my sister will do living on her own washes over me. How often will I be able to see her? Will she fall further into her addiction if I'm not there to keep her in check?

I'm disappointed, too, over the lack of privacy I now have. I can't help but think of that as Ellis holds open the door to my room. Gasping, I cover my mouth. I struggle to take a step forward as my eyes absorb the stunning space.

"Is there a problem? Christopher said you prefer light colors, but if he misunderstood, we'll have it changed. The interior decorator is prompt to respond to my needs."

The luxurious bedroom is adorned in the colors of white and champagne. New furniture, with an antique feel, graces the room, and the bedding is too expensive to touch.

"It's beautiful and extravagant. I–I can't do this. It's too bizarre. Please let Liam and me go." I turn to flee, but Ellis grabs my bicep and spins me around, slamming the door closed behind me with the force of his strong hand.

In a beat, I'm against his chest, staring at another crimson tie, one brighter than he wore to Tony's visitation.

"Look at me." His fingers lift my chin to give me no other choice, so I close my eyes in defiance. "I said look at me, Camilla." Huffing, I open them back up. God, his rich blue portals puncture me with depth and fortitude.

"We had an agreement, and you're not going anywhere. This will be an adjustment for everyone, but I'm doing what I can to make you comfortable. At least in *most* areas you'll be comfortable."

"What do you mean by most?"

"I'm thirty-four and haven't met a woman I see a future with. I'm tired of searching. I hate dating. And as I previously stated, I want Liam growing up here, so it seems like a perfect arrangement for you to meet my sexual needs in exchange for the security I can provide you."

"That makes me a prostitute."

"Let's call it companionship. You won't have financial worries, and Liam will receive the best care and education. You won't have to pay for the remainder of yours, either."

"Maybe you don't want to date again, but did you ever consider that I might want another man in my life?"

"Six empty bottles of pills were found next to Tony's dead body. Did you know he took his own life?"

"No," I whisper as I look to the floor.

"You withheld from my brother that he had a son, and I believe he'd be here today if you hadn't. I guess you've forgotten how fast I can destroy your life and take Liam. If you take that into account, this should seem like a generous term."

I wish I could tell him Tony knew about Liam and chose not to have anything to do with his son, but I've already said he didn't, and I don't know what would happen if I confessed the truth about Christopher. What if it blew up in my face, and I lost Liam?

Besides, I have a feeling it wouldn't change a thing. Ellis made his decision and has the upper hand no matter what.

"So, I would have sex with you when you want it?"

He inhales, and it's as if he sucked in some of the sexual tension floating in the air around us. It quickly settles like fog in his gaze.

The lust is clouding my vision, as well, and apparently my better judgment, since my nipples are hardening beneath my blouse, rising up to weigh in on whether we can despise Ellis at the same time he bends us over that magnificent king-size bed.

"Actually, it's more involved than that." Sliding an arm around my waist, he pulls me even closer, and I feel his cock thickening against my pelvis.

"You're going to be my submissive."

"What? No, I–I can't do something like that." My attempt to break free from his hold is futile as he strengthens his grip. He's much taller than me, probably six foot four, yet I can feel his scorching breath on my face.

The scent of every part of him is drawing me in, from his aftershave to his minty breath, or maybe it's some sort of pheromones that are causing my irrational behavior where I'm envisioning what he's asking of me ... of what he might want to do to me.

"You can and you will if you don't want to lose—"

"Don't bring Liam into this. Anything else but not this," I snap, poking his chest.

Without warning, his fingers press into the back of my neck, and he slams his lips to mine. He tries to push his tongue in, but I don't let him.

His fingertips apply more pressure, the act so primal and dominating that I relent. Just like that, my mouth opens for him, giving him exactly what he wants.

His groan sails between my lips before his tongue assaults mine. Sharp and precise strokes are like a strike to a match, igniting my dormant sexual needs, the arousal gripping my senses. My skin flushes, and as blood swooshes to my ears, the sound of my heartbeat chimes in as the chorus.

Unexpectedly, he releases my lips, and although it seems sudden, I can't help but wonder if it was actually a lengthy kiss I was utterly lost in.

His strong hand moves from my neck to my thick hair, and he gathers it into a ponytail before tugging downward, lifting my eyes and chin to meet his penetrating stare.

"You..." he says in a breathy tone. "I'm going to pleasure your body and inflict pain on you until you're splintered down to your soul. Stripped bare and kneeling at my feet, you'll beg me not to stop. To never let you go."

"Please, Ellis. I can't. I have to be in control at all times. I *have* to be."

While still clutching my hair, he makes quick work of undoing my jeans. "What's happening?" I ask. Jerking my pants open, he shoves his hand in the front of my panties. His fingers push inside me, and I whimper from the pleasurable intrusion.

"You're not going anywhere because you're a fucking liar. You're dripping wet for me, so I feel no remorse. If we were truly alone, I'd already have you on your knees with my cock buried in your throat. Be ready because I'm coming back for you."

He storms from the room, and I drop to the plush carpeting, my body limp from being shaken to its core.

To drown out a sob, I cover my mouth, but could anyone even hear me? I'm sitting in a mansion, where most of the rooms are far apart, and I'm not close to Liam's, which I hate.

Feeling a dire need to be with my little boy, I jump to my feet and hurry to a door in my bedroom that I suspect leads to a bathroom.

Once inside, I grab tissues from a fancy container on the vanity and wipe my eyes. My face is pink and puffy, and there's no doubt Chris will know something's wrong. I have to be strong for Liam, but I'm already failing to draw on that strength.

I have to find it.

Quietly, I pad to Liam's room, and with trepidation, I peek around the doorway, hoping Ellis isn't present. Seeing that Christopher and Liam are alone, I walk in and shut the door behind me.

Chris must see the agony in my eyes since he jumps up from where he's been playing on the floor with Liam. I sling my arms around his neck and hug him, needing to believe he's still my friend.

I've survived many stressful, disturbing events in my life, but this one is kicking my ass early in the game.

Pulling back, he grasps my shoulders, and his expression is one of concern as he surveys my face.

"What happened? What did he say to you?"

"It's—it's OK. I'm overwhelmed, is all."

"Tell me what he said."

"He reinforced what I already knew; he'll be calling the shots. I feel owned, and I'm confused about so many things. I want out of here."

His thumb brushes a tear away from my cheek.

"My offer still stands, Cammy," he whispers. "I'll give up this job in a heartbeat if you'll leave here and be with me. Maybe over time, your feelings will change. I've waited this long to have you, and I'll wait longer if need be."

Shaking my head no, I pull away. Pressure over something else is not what I need right now.

"I can't. The day might come when I flee from this place like a tornado is chasing me, but right now I'm too scared of losing Liam. It's not a chance I can take.

"My hope is that Ellis will grow tired of us being here and let me leave. Like you said, he's not used to having a woman and child in his home."

"I'm getting you and Liam out of here one way or another. You'll see."

"Momma, I'm hungry," Liam says, tugging on my pant leg.

"Crap, what time is it?"

Chris pulls his phone from his pocket.

"2:30."

"We've missed lunch, and he's normally down for a nap at this time. It's our first day here, and I'm already neglecting Liam."

"Stop, he's fine. We'll go to the kitchen and feed him something. Then, I'll have Irene make an early dinner. Take some deep breaths, OK?"

Nodding, I start to pick Liam up, but with my back already hurting, I take his hand instead.

Reaching the top of the staircase, I shudder from the thought of how Ellis's office is just to my left.

On the tour, Chris said it's the only room to the right as you're coming up the stairs. All the bedrooms, including Liam's and mine, are at the opposite end of the hallway.

Starting down the stairs, I show Liam how to hold the intricately designed railing with his right hand, and I give strict orders that he is never to be alone on the staircase.

It feels like an eternity before we get down the winding masterpiece of architecture. Liam's cute in his little jeans and white tennis shoes, taking each step so carefully. He's a touch fearful, and I hope it stays that way.

"I can't get over this place," I utter to Chris while we sit at the dining room table that probably seats sixteen. I'm not counting the damn chairs.

"I hate to ask Ellis for anything, but if he wants to save this expensive rug beneath us, he should put a small dinette set in the kitchen for Liam to eat at. There's plenty of space for one."

"I can ask him."

"Liam also needs a booster seat. The poor kid's eyes barely see over the top of this cherry table. He probably wonders where the television is and the TV trays we always eat from are."

After popping a grape inside his mouth, my kid studies another one he's holding in his hand. Lowering my voice, I whisper, "He's quiet. I hope he'll be able to adjust."

"He will. He's got both of us, and I'm sure the nanny will be great, too."

Sighing, I stare out the windows facing the back of the property. The sun is shining over the snow-covered lawn, making it glisten.

I notice a couple of men in coveralls entering and exiting what appears to be a guest house. One is holding a ladder, and from the look of things, the guys are doing some kind of maintenance inside the grey brick building.

"Are you moving in back there?" I ask Chris. "February seems like an odd time to be doing construction."

"*Ellis* is odd," he mumbles. "No. Mr. Burke won't share with me what he's having done to the place, and he was adamant I never go near it. Those men have been working since I started."

"Interesting." I help Liam with the last bite of his ham sandwich, and he dusts his hands off in his lap. "I guess I need to ask Irene to vacuum under the table daily, too."

"Don't worry so much. Ellis needs to see what he's getting himself into with wanting to help raise Liam. He's not cut out for this."

Realizing he's talking loudly, Chris glances around to ensure we're still alone. My kiddo yawns, drawing my attention back to him.

"I hate for Liam to nap this late in the afternoon, but he'll be a horrible dinner guest if he doesn't get at least a small one in. I'm taking him to my room. Where is Ellis, anyway?"

"I believe in his office. From what I've gathered, he's a workaholic."

"That's a relief. Maybe we'll see less of him because of it."

Ellis

Christopher steps inside my office and shuts the door behind him.

"In the future, you need to ask before you barge in here."

"Right, sorry. Liam had lunch and is napping. Irene's fixing an early dinner since I couldn't get Camilla to eat anything." His gaze shifts to the floor. "It seems whatever you two discussed upset her."

Glowering, I lean back in my chair. He's really butting into my business, and I don't like it; however, for now I'll bite my tongue on this matter, which is not an easy task for me.

"Thank you. I'll talk to Ms. Rose, and please tell Irene I'll have my meal in my office. You're welcome to stay for dinner before you head out this evening."

"Sure. Thank you." He hesitates, so I raise my eyebrows. "Is there something else you'd like to say?"

"No, that's all." Exerting a breath, he turns and leaves. What was that about? There was obviously something else, and he held his tongue.

Curious as to what Camilla shared with him, I set out to find her. As I stroll down the hallway, I look over the half wall and spot Christopher reaching the bottom of the staircase.

I come to a stop at Liam's room on the right and find his full-size bed still neatly made. Where the hell is he? Striding farther down the hallway, passing a guest room and what will be Camilla's study, I reach her bedroom.

No one answers after I knock twice, so I crack open her door. She sits right up in bed, still fully clothed, and I notice Liam asleep next to her.

Dammit. He's not sleeping in here.

"I want a word with you."

Rolling her eyes, she climbs out of bed and pads toward me. Following me into the hallway, she pulls the door until it's only cracked behind her.

"What do you need?"

"Why is he in your bed?"

"He always sleeps with me."

"He's three and needs to be sleeping in his own room. Do you want him to grow up weak, or would you like to see a strong, independent man?"

"Jesus christ, Ellis. Look, I've never had an extra bedroom, so this is all he knows. I can't toss him into this new environment and also expect him to sleep alone in a room he's not familiar with. He'll be terrified."

"Well, I'm going to want you alone with *me* soon at night, so he has to get comfortable in his own bed. I'm giving you three days to get him acclimated to his room.

"I purchased monitors so you can see and listen to him, and the nanny will care for him when you're with me." I hold up three fingers. "You get three days, Camilla. I mean it."

She crosses her arms. "You're a coldhearted ass."

"And you just earned a paddling to yours." I turn to leave, but I recall two more things I wanted to speak to her about.

"Oh, and don't be confiding in Christopher about our personal business unless you want him fired. Lastly, you need to eat all of your meals. I don't want you to become sick from lack of proper nourishment."

"Yes, I'm sure you'd hate for me to disrupt your twisted plans to torture me."

"For that comment you're getting a taste of it tomorrow."

"But you said I had three days."

"We'll fit it in."

CHAPTER SEVEN

Camilla

"I want to hire Emma," I say, sitting in a chair across from Ellis's desk. "She's young, so she can keep up with Liam, yet she's educated, too, having graduated from college last year." I don't even think he's listening to me as he stares at my chest. "She's light and happy, and I think—"

"Why are you wearing a different shirt?" he interjects.

I glance down at the red sweater I changed into after the interviews.

"I spilled coffee on my other one."

Tightening his hand around an ink pen atop his cherry desk, his eyes flit to a matching credenza on his right. I look to it and notice he's eyeing a red abstract sculpture of a woman.

"I'm hiring Beatrice," he says curtly. "She'll be stricter with Liam, which he obviously needs since you're determined to baby him."

"You don't know how I am with him; we've been here a whole twenty-four hours. Beatrice was stuffy and would have a difficult time relating to Liam. She couldn't chase him around this enormous house, either."

With his elbows resting on the desk, Ellis palms his eyes.

"You're trying my patience."

Yes, he's about to cave. I feel it.

"Emma could tutor him, too. You said you wanted him to have a tutor until he goes to preschool next fall, so this way, you wouldn't have to hire an additional person."

"Emma doesn't speak any foreign languages."

I make a face, wondering what that has to do with anything.

"How is that relevant?"

"Liam is learning other languages."

"Well, how many do you speak?"

"I can read eight and speak six. It's a must with my job."

Crap, so much for working that angle.

"Ellis, please let me make this decision. Mothers have an intuition, and my gut is telling me Emma is perfect for the job."

Dropping his hands, he stares at me. His eyes aren't as vibrant today. Instead they're a little bloodshot, and he appears tired, which I can relate to seeing how I was up for hours trying to keep Liam in his own bed.

It was a futile attempt. He was determined to win, his cries gut-wrenching. After close to two hours of listening to him wail, I couldn't take it any longer and brought him back to my bedroom.

"I'll think about it, but I need you to go now. I have an appointment."

"On a Saturday? Do you always work on the weekend?"

"It's not work related. Oh, and Irene is only here until one on Saturdays, and she's off every Sunday, but I have her working all this weekend since you're settling in.

"She'll help with Liam if needed, and she loves to cook, so she'll fix you anything at any time."

"Thank you. I guess Liam and I will spend the day getting more acquainted with your home."

"It's your home, as well, Camilla, and we'll adjust sooner if you treat it as such. I want my nephew to feel he belongs here."

"And this mansion is not going to feel like home to me in a day, especially when I've been sentenced to jail."

"Oh, please, this is far from jail. Liam being a Burke means his life is forever changed. The opportunities and wealth he's entitled to are endless, so I'm trying to give you somewhat of the same opportunity since you're his mother."

I don't have a reply. On one hand he seems like a generous man, but then I recall what Tony divulged about him, along with what Ellis expects from me in return for this luxurious life, and I'm conflicted. Standing, I cross my arms.

"I do hope you'll consider Emma for the job. It would mean a lot to me."

I leave his office to spend time with my son. Having been in more dangerous situations than this, I need to focus on the silver lining, which is the possibility of Liam having better opportunities in life and less struggles. That is, as long as Ellis isn't the evil person I believe him to be.

I find Liam in his room, where Christopher's watching him.

"Everything OK?" Chris asks.

"Yes, it's fine. I'm hoping Ellis will hire the nanny I want. He's going to think about it."

"He better. You know what's best for Liam. Ellis texted me to come see him, so I better go. Irene already fed Liam lunch. You should eat something, too, and check out the family room

I showed you downstairs. There's a flat-screen TV and a lot of movies Liam would like."

"OK. I appreciate all of your help. It's comforting."

He pulls my forehead to him and kisses it.

"I'll do anything for you. You know that."

Unsure of how to respond, I simply smile and pick up Liam to go downstairs. Not having an appetite, I head right for the spacious family room.

There's an enormous entertainment center taking up the wall across from a brown leather sectional, so I open the doors to it and spot stacks of DVDs, especially children's movies. I pull some from the shelf and bend down to show them to Liam.

"Wanna watch a movie, kiddo? Pick one, and I'll play it." I already know the answer to this. One of the three DVDs I'm holding is a *Ninja Turtles* movie, so he'll surely pick that one. He grins and points to it.

"I *Mikey*."

"Yes, you're *Michelangelo*."

Shooting his arms in the air, he says, "*Cowabunga*! I need chucks, Momma." He's serious now, certain that one of these days he'll persuade me to buy them.

"I think you're still a little young for nunchucks. You'd whack yourself in the head. Let's sit on the sofa and watch the movie."

As we lounge, I dwell on how this is the only place in the house that feels casual besides Liam's bedroom.

I can tuck my feet up beside me on the sofa, which gives me the sense of being at *my* home. It wasn't much, but I paid the rent and decided whether to live there or not.

I sigh from annoyance over the predicament we're in. I prefer that Liam not watch much television, but I see us spending a lot of time in here as a reprieve from Ellis and this lavish environment.

***

Close to two hours have passed when Christopher enters the room. Liam is napping on my lap, and the movie is off. I've been playing on my iPhone, wondering the whole time if Ellis is monitoring every keystroke.

"Hi, what's up? I've heard a lot of commotion in the house," I say.

Blowing out a breath, he grabs the back of his neck.

"You need to go to your room."

"Why?"

"Ellis purchased a bunch of clothes for you and Liam. They were even delivered. I guess the man's money gets him whatever the fuck he desires, including Saturday delivery—"

"Shhh, watch your language, even if it appears he's sleeping." I glance down at Liam.

"Sorry. I didn't know how you'd like them organized, so Liam's are on his bed, and yours are, well, everywhere in your room. There's a lot.

"I can't lie; it pisses me off. You've never taken help from me, so it's irritating that he gets to do this, and you have to accept it."

"I don't have a choice, and I hate it. You, of all people, know I'm used to being independent."

"I'll watch Liam while you're upstairs. Then, I'm taking off for the day. I've had enough of Ellis Burke this week."

"I'm sorry. Thank you again for all your help."

Ellis

My heels dig in the mat as I grapple to get Dean in a rear naked choke. His back's to my chest as I shove my hips upward and crank down harder on his neck. He's going to tap. I feel it.

In seconds, he smacks my forearm three times fast like I knew he would. He wore me the hell out. We both sit up, breathing harshly, and it irritates me that this isn't as easy as it was ten years ago, when I was twenty-four.

"Damn, what the hell has you so fired up? You're a bear today," my trainer says before he lifts his t-shirt to wipe sweat from his face. He pats down his dark hair next.

I can't tell him there's a woman in my house, wearing red, who has my head so fucked up that it leaves me wanting to fuck someone else up. I can't ravish her the way I'd like to at the moment, so this has to be the next best thing to lessen my frustration.

"I don't want to talk about it today." Peeling my shirt away from my skin, I toss it aside on the blue mat.

"All right, then maybe we need to go out soon and discuss it instead of you trying to kill me."

"Can you not handle it? Are you calling yourself a pussy?"

Yanking his soaked shirt off, he smacks me with it, and I laugh. My eyes meet the glass door of my gym, and I spot Camilla staring. She moves out of sight, so I spring to my feet and head for the door. Opening it, I see her scurrying away.

"Stop. What do you need?"

"I can talk to you about it later. I'm sorry I was watching."

"Turn around, Camilla." She shifts to face me, and staring at the ground, she bites her lip. "Come inside. We were just finishing up." Nodding, she follows me into the gym.

"Dean, this is Camilla. Camilla, this is my friend, and jiujitsu trainer, Dean."

"Give me a second," he says with a smile. He jogs over to his gym bag, and pulling out a clean shirt, he yanks it over his head and hurries back. He's such a gentleman. Asshole. He sticks out his hand to shake Camilla's. "It's nice to meet you."

"Likewise." Camilla's eyes look around the space that's filled with typical gym equipment.

"I'll show you out," I say to Dean, knowing he has questions. I glance to Camilla first. "Wait here." Once Dean and I are in the hallway, he turns to me wearing a shit-eating grin.

"I see what's got you worked up now. She's hot, man."

"Yeah, and she's living here, too."

His eyes bulge. "What the fuck? I didn't even know you were dating someone."

"It's a long story."

"That I'm dying to hear. Just message me, and we'll grab dinner next week." He holds his hand up to grip mine, and we swat each other's back as a farewell. "I can let myself out. It seems you have something more exciting to attend to."

"Thanks for the workout." Dean leaves, and I stroll back in the gym to face the woman in red. I don't need another one occupying my head at night.

Camilla

The room smells of sweat and Ellis. It would probably seem pungent to most, but his manly scent of lemongrass and earth is overpowering the space.

It's like that first aroma of spring, igniting the senses, where we have a renewed hope of possibilities for the year after a hibernating winter. And I must say, the possibilities of what could happen between Ellis and me this spring seem endless.

"I hope you didn't stop because of me."

"We were finished. I train with him every Saturday if time allows it."

"It was impressive, and there have been a few times in my life when moves like that would've come in handy."

His brow cinches. "What did you need?"

"I wanted to thank you for the clothing and accessories. I could combine all the purses and pairs of shoes I've owned in my life, and they wouldn't add up to the number now in my walk-in closet.

"And evening gowns… I can't imagine what I need those for. You should know I'm simple. It doesn't take much to make me happy."

"Who said I'm trying to make you happy?"

"That's not what I meant. I mean—forget it, I'll go." I turn to leave, but he grabs me and brings me close. His slick arm brushes along mine, and I shudder as his sweaty body moves closer. Fuck, I imagine him being the baby oil to my bare skin. He's too much man for me.

"You're welcome," he utters, "and now I'm going to kiss you for not being after my money like every other damn woman I've dated."

"Who said I'm trying to date you?" I chime, smirking.

"Clever."

I shrug. "You had it coming." A foot sweeps my leg, knocking mine out from under me. Holding my back and head, Ellis takes me straight to the mat next to us.

He's on top of me as I stare up wide-eyed, heaving for a breath. "How did that not hurt me?"

He smirks, and I have the urge to press my thumb to his sexy dimpled chin.

"I know what I'm doing, that's how. Now, shut up, clever woman." His lips slam to mine, and his tongue forces its way inside.

This kiss is Patrón on the rocks, rimmed with the thickest salt. His tongue's the lime, and in a hot second, I'm drunk from arousal, wishing I were naked so I could feel his slick-with-sweat body slide over mine.

Reveling in the salt and heat and sweat and muscle, I moan into the devil's pit of flames. A mouth so hot and tempting.

My body wants to fornicate, whereas my mind recites Corinthians, verse something or other, about temptation, but holy shit, this is too hot to obey the Bible.

Dragging my nails down his back, I open my legs for him. He shoves between them, and his iron-hard cock presses through his thin workout pants. It's aligned with my pussy, and my jeans cause an ache as they rub against my flesh.

He growls inside my mouth before he pulls away.

NO, come back. I choose fornication.

"We can't do this here." He nods his head to the side. "The see-through door. Damn, with you around, it's hard to remember there's a kid here, too."

He climbs off of me and reaches out his hand to help me up. I'm lightheaded, still intoxicated from his drugging kiss. "I need a shower. I'm counting the nights, my Rose. Counting. Them. Down."

Swiping his shirt off the floor, he struts to the door, his back still glistening, and I'm left behind in his wake of pheromones.

CHAPTER EIGHT

Ellis

I stride to the kitchen Sunday morning and only find Irene cooking. The house is too quiet.

"Where is Camilla and Liam?"

"They haven't come down yet, sir."

I glance at my watch. It's 9:30 a.m., and I don't know much about children, but I was certain they woke up early. I paid Irene to be here today so she could serve Camilla and Liam meals, yet they're not even down for breakfast.

"I'll go find them."

Liam is not in his bed when I crack open his door, so I roll my eyes. *Not this shit again.* Irritated, I march to Camilla's room, and after tapping on the door, I open it. She shoots up in bed, much like the first day she was here, and looks at her alarm clock.

"Can you please wait for me to answer next time instead of barging in my room?"

"I told you how I felt about Liam sleeping in here."

"Did you not hear him last night? He cried and yelled for hours. He finally fell asleep at midnight, but he woke up again at two this morning and threw another fit. I didn't know what else to do, so I had to bring him in here to get some rest."

With a long yawn, Liam sits up in bed, and his hair is in total disarray, poking out everywhere. I begin to smile but quickly recover my scowl.

71

"After thirty minutes of his wailing, I put in earplugs."

Her head cocks to the side in a *fuck-you* manner.

"How lucky for you. What did you want?"

"I'm paying Irene to be here today for the two of you, so could you please come downstairs so she can serve breakfast? I saw her making pancakes. They're the best."

Liam claps. "I want pancakes, Momma."

"Why does he call you that? Why not mother or even mom?"

"How many times do I have to remind you he's three? And I'm sure your investigative skills disclosed I'm from the south. Did you honestly call your mom *mother* at three years old?"

"I believe so. I was taught to call her mother."

Camilla grips her hip. "Well, that's sad to me."

I huff. "Just come downstairs. We'll eat together in the dining room."

Camilla

Breakfast is as awkward as I suspected it would be. Ellis squirms each time Liam slings syrup or drips it down the front of his own shirt.

While nibbling on his bacon, my curious kid stares Ellis down, and I have to get us out of this uncomfortable situation. The silence might as well be nails on a chalkboard.

"I'm going to give this sticky kid a bath," I say. Liam smacks his hands together, and they stick, so he yanks, trying to get them apart. Glancing to Ellis, I actually see him smile.

"I have something I want to show you after. Irene will watch Liam."

"OK. After I shower, I'll find you."

***

I'm unsure if it's the sugary pancakes that have me nauseous or the anticipation of what Ellis has in store for me, but I suck it up and tap on his open office door.

"Hi. You said you had something to show me?"

Leaning back in his chair, he laces his fingers behind his head, forcing me to admire him in his black button-up shirt. Even beneath the dark color, I can see the shape of his fit arms. He's eyeing me intently, his gaze trailing down my body.

"What should I do with you?" he asks under his breath.

Oh, shit.

Rising from his desk, he strides around it with purpose and grabs my hand. "Come with me." Leading me down the hallway toward my bedroom, he stops at the door before it and opens it.

"Chris didn't show me this room. What's in it?"

"Your study. You'll need a place to do your schoolwork for that worthless degree you're determined to get."

Snatching my hand away, I follow him inside, and the door shuts behind us.

"And as I said before, it's not worthless." Like when I first saw my bedroom, I'm stunned and in awe over the decorated space. "Ellis..."

Taking a few steps forward, I admire a beautiful white desk in the back center of the room. It sits on an oriental rug covering the light cherry wood floor.

On my right are two darling yellow wingback chairs in front of rows of bookshelves that rest against the wall. There are tall shelves to the left, as well, every one of them filled with books.

The study is painted a milky white, and splashes of yellow décor light up the space. It's cheerful, airy and adds to the array of mixed signals from Mr. Ellis Burke.

"I didn't know what you liked to read, so I purchased a variety of genres. There are classics, along with new novels, but Christopher will order whatever you like."

"Thank you. Like my bedroom, and the clothing, this is all too much." Wandering over to the desk, I run my fingers along the solid piece of wood.

"Oh, and a new laptop and printer are being set up tomorrow." Turning back to him, I smile, but it dissipates when I recall his job.

"You're getting those so you can spy on me."

If looks could kill, this one would do the trick. He charges toward me.

"Young lady, it wouldn't matter if you kept that piece of shit laptop of yours. I can get inside any computer in seconds."

"I, I'm sorry. I wasn't trying to seem ungrateful."

"Right. You're only determined to piss me off. If you think being difficult is going to make me change my terms, you can think again. You mouthing off to me only makes me want to punish you more. Don't move." He strides to the door and locks it.

"I should check on Liam," I say.

"He's fine with Irene."

Heading back to me, I see the lust surfacing in his gaze. He clutches my hand and pulls me around my desk where he takes a seat in my new tan leather chair.

For the first time, I'm staring down at him. His hungry eyes tilt up at me, and I suck in a breath. "Strip off your pants, and get down on your knees."

"I don't want to," I whisper unconvincingly since I'm all kinds of fucked up in the head and have no clue what I want.

"Bullshit. I'm going to tell you one more time, Camilla, and if you don't do as I say, I'm going to lay you over this desk and spank you ... *hard*. Now, remove your pants, and kneel in front of me."

Swallowing, I unzip my skinny jeans. "Take your panties off, too." Kicking off my flats, I remove everything he asked me to and lower to my knees in front of him.

"Your blouse and bra—off." My hands shake as I bring them up and fumble on the first button. "I want your eyes on mine."

On a deep inhale, I steady my fingers and look up at him. His tongue sweeps over his bottom lip, and once I've undone the last button on my light blue blouse, his gaze drops to my chest. I push the shirt over my shoulders, and before I can let it fall, he swipes it from me.

My trembling increases as I reach behind my back and undo my lace bra. I drop it to the floor and watch him as he rolls my blouse up into one long, thin piece of fabric. "I'm blindfolding you now."

Placing the cloth over my eyes, he ties it securely behind my head. I'm vulnerable, sucking in short breaths and shaking as beads of sweat form above my lip.

"I sense you've never been blindfolded before."

"No."

"Good." Not being able to see, my ears hone in on the sound of his belt buckle being undone. I hear the zipper of his jeans slowly lower next, and it incites a chill that skirts across my bare skin. I hate him, so why am I itching with excitement and wonderment?

It sounds like Ellis sits back down in front of me.

"Give me your hand," he orders. I lift my right one, and he takes hold of it. "My Rose ... you're going to stroke my dick, and then you're going to suck it until I come in your mouth."

Gasping, I start to swipe my hand away, but he clamps down on it. "I'm going to ask you a question, and if you're honest with me, I'll ensure you come, too. Do you want to suck my cock?"

"No." The word flies from my lips.

"Hmm ... I think you have a problem with lying."

"I'm not lying. I never agreed to a *term* like this."

I flinch when his fingers graze my stomach and continue moving downward.

"Last chance to tell the truth. Your pussy's going to give you away."

"I'm not saying it." In an instant, his fingers push inside me, and dammit, it happens with ease.

"You dirty little liar. Your cunt is soaked with need, but you're too damn stubborn to admit it. Fine. You can hang on to all that sexual tension. It can build and build, but one day soon, you're going to beg me to give you a release."

His fingers glide in and out of me, and the sound of my juices moving with them fills the smoldering air. "I know you hear that magnificent sound. Mmm ... your pussy's wet, warm and tight around my digits."

Whimpering, I sink onto his fingers and scold myself for enjoying the sensations. "I'll give you one more chance. Tell me you want this, and I'll continue until you come."

"No. I won't say it, and you can't make me." He stops pleasuring me, and I soon feel how wet his fingers are as he uses them to wrap my hand around his cock. *Shit.*

I stroke it, noticing its wide girth and how smooth yet hard it is inside my palm.

"You're right, I can't make you, but if you haven't noticed, you're stroking my cock on your own free will."

I consider stopping... I do, but I don't stop, and it's because this is the hottest fucking moment I've ever experienced in my life.

I didn't think he could top the sweaty rendezvous in his gym yesterday, but this is winning. As much as my personality is screaming at me not to let him boss me, I'm discovering I like it.

Running his fingers through my hair, he massages my scalp until my head falls back and lips part for air. "Put your mouth over my cock. Do it now and *suck*."

The emphasis of his last filthy word directs me to do as he commands. My head leans over, and I take his entire long length inside my mouth. In unison with a hiss, he flinches and clamps down on my hair.

"Yes, like that." He's moving my head for me, so I focus on stroking him with one hand while grazing his balls with the other. His pelvis thrusts upward, burying his cock farther back in my throat. I try to relax it so as not to gag.

He's so big, and I keep imagining what his dick looks like and how it would feel deep inside me. Pulling back, I trace the tip of the head with my tongue. He groans and shoves my lips back over it.

I move my mouth faster, up and down, sucking him off until he grunts and stiffens. He comes inside my mouth, and the thick liquid shoots violently to the back of my throat until finally, I swallow it down.

Every–damn–drop, like it was made only for me to drink. I've been thinking he's the sick fuck, but it's me. I'm excited over giving him head when he's blackmailing me to live in his home against my will.

Pulling on my arm, he signals for me to stand. I'm wobbly until I feel his tongue roll over my nipple. My hands find his shoulders, and I use them to brace myself as he sucks the stiff pebble inside his mouth.

"Yes," I say breathlessly. His fingers thrust inside me, and my legs open to give him room. I'm loving every sensation, from his heated mouth to his thick fingers stretching my walls. "Oh, please don't stop." As I pant for air and dig my nails into his shoulders, his fingers slip from me.

No!

"Stand still." He moves around me, stirring up a breeze, and it sounds like he's fastening his pants. Shortly after, he removes the blindfold. My hand shields my eyes as they snap shut from the intrusive light.

"Let this serve as a lesson not to lie to me. Open your eyes." I do, and I'm confronted with his penetrating gaze. He's fully clothed, holding my blouse in his hand. "You can make our years together easy, or you can make them hard. It's up to you."

Grabbing my shirt from him, I hold it over my exposed breasts.

"*Years...?* Do you even hear yourself? You're a handsome and wealthy man who could have as many women in your bed as you choose, probably at once even, yet you're trying to play house with me in some twisted way."

"I've already had a *plethora* of women, and like we've discussed repeatedly, I want you and Liam here so he can be raised as a Burke."

"Now, you're lying. You didn't bring us here so you could get close to Liam. You brought us here because of your desire to use me.

"You said you were pissed I withheld from Tony that he had a son, but I think you're doing this to feel like you own what was once his, and it's all because you hated him as much as he hated you."

Turning beet red with anger, he points his finger in my face.

"I have *never* felt hatred toward my brother, and you're lying to yourself if you think Tony gave a damn about you. Not once did he breathe your fucking name to me."

Tears come, but I hold them at bay. I don't know why his words sting. I learned years ago that Tony didn't give two shits for me, and Christopher confirmed he didn't care about Liam, either.

"You're evil, and although my body may betray me and desire your touch, my heart holds only contempt for you. Get out so I can dress and care for my son."

"It's your last night, Camilla. Tomorrow, I'm turning your ass scarlet." He storms out, and if I wasn't so pissed, I'd be a pile on the floor like my clothing.

The man is all over the place with his behavior and moods, and I'm angry because as much as I wish to hate him, I can't. He has a reason to feel this desperation.

He doesn't remember me, but in the dark trenches of his psyche, he knows I've wronged him, so he's unleashing on me what his subconscious is telling him I deserve.

I let out a clipped laugh. The man was about to commit treason all those years ago, yet I'm the one feeling guilty and justifying his actions. It's so typical of me.

CHAPTER NINE

Ellis

For fuck's sake that kid has a set of lungs on him.

Sitting up at the side of my bed, I pull on a pair of sweats, yawning as I go. I stagger out to the hallway and let the noise steer me. As I stroll closer to Liam's room, I realize it's not only his cries I'm hearing.

Camilla is huddled up in a ball on the floor outside his door, and she's crying right along with him. *Fuck.* My chest constricts, and a foreign feeling grabs hold of me. Squatting down next to her, I pat her shoulder.

"Camilla, sit up." Like it takes all the effort in the world, she drags herself up and leans back against the wall. Her heart is breaking over his cries, and what I can't handle, or even understand, is the fact mine is breaking, too, over the sounds from both of them.

Moving her wet auburn hair from her face, I then use my hands to wipe away some of her tears. "I'll handle this," I say. Her arms wrap around my leg as I go to stand.

"No, you'll scare him."

"I promise I'll be nice." I remove her hands from my leg. "You have to trust me. If you come in, he's never going to stop this."

"If he cries louder, I'm getting him."

Squatting down again, I cup her face.

"The U.S. government trusts me with their most classified documents. I think you can trust me with my own nephew." I shouldn't have shared that, but I'm also half asleep and annoyed that she finds me incapable of caring for him.

I crack his door open, and he stops wailing. Thinking it's best not to turn on the overhead light, I walk over to the dresser to my right and click on a table lamp.

"Momma," he whines from his bed in the middle of the room. As he adjusts his eyes to the light, he sniffles and coughs. The second those blue irises meet mine, they grow to the size of saucers. "I want my momma."

"It's all right, little guy. Your mom is sleeping. You don't want to wake her, do you?" He stares oddly at me, probably thinking *hell, yeah, I do* and debating on whether to yell *stranger danger.* I guess he doesn't know what that means, but I should teach him.

"I thought we'd read a story. Would you like that?" Not waiting for him to tell me no, I walk over to the short bookshelf next to the head of his bed. Pulling out two books, I hold them up in front of him.

"You get to pick."

Smiling faintly, he points to ... what the hell? *The Poky Little Puppy*? "Damn, kid, you do need a male role model. *Moby Dick* was probably being read to me by your age. OK, then. I guess we're reading about a poky puppy," I murmur.

Glancing around the room, I spot a rocking chair in the corner, so I drag it over next to his bed. "Can I sit here so you can turn the pages for me?"

Still looking like he's weighing whether or not to scream, he hesitates before nodding. I'm about to read the first page when I stop and look at him. "Do you remember my name?"

His finger goes into his mouth as he shakes his head no. His eyes fill with fear, like he'll be in trouble for not remembering.

"That's OK. It's Ellis, but why don't we think of a name that will be easier for you to remember? First, what's your name? Is it Bob?"

Liam smiles and shakes his head, but he shuts that shit down fast as he recalls I'm still the stranger next to his bed. "Oh, right, it's not Bob, it's Carl."

He smiles wider this time, his head shaking, and now we're making progress. "If it's not Carl or Bob, what is it then?"

"Liam," he whispers. His blue eyes stare back at mine, and it's as if I'm looking in a mirror. The kid couldn't favor a Burke more.

"My uncle has a name that only I get to call him because, well, I'm his favorite nephew. Uncle Rich. Do you want a name to call me that no one else can use?"

He nods, and I wonder if he gets what I'm saying. "Um, let me think..." I consider Z for my middle name, Zander, but I find it more amusing to come up with a nickname Camilla will hate. Boss, maybe? Yes. She'll hate it, and I'll love hearing it.

"You can call me Boss, and you'll be the only one."

He grins, this time showing me his miniature teeth.

"Boss," he says.

"Do you have a nickname you want me to call you?"

Tilting his eyes to the ceiling, he smiles bashfully and shakes his head.

"That's OK. I'll keep calling you Bob until you think of one."

He giggles loudly, and I can't help but laugh, too.

"OK, let's get back to this poky puppy. I'll make a deal with you; if you go to sleep after the story and stay in your big-boy bed all night, I'll read you another book tomorrow. Do we have a deal?"

Still flashing me a smile, he nods and settles comfortably in his bed. He seems at ease, and even yawns, as I start the book. Maybe I'm not so *diabolical*, as Camilla put it.

Camilla

I bite on my nails, waiting to hear another noise from Liam's room. I'd settled down after discovering how amazing Ellis was treating him, but now it's quiet in there, and I'm wondering why.

The door slowly opens, and Ellis slips out. I jump to my feet and look at him. A lamp on a table at the end of the hallway emits enough light for me to see his attractive face and sexy bedhead hair.

"He's asleep, and I don't think he'll cry again tonight. You should go back to bed."

"Thank you."

"It was nothing."

"I was actually thinking of going downstairs to find a snack. Want to join me?" I shouldn't have asked. We can't get along for more than five minutes. Oh, and I hate him—I think. But his kindness and patience toward my little one has tugged on my heart-strings.

Staring down at me, he scratches the back of his head, likely wondering, too, if it's the best idea.

"All right. Lead the way." As we take the stairs, I imagine how bad I must look, so I comb my fingers through my hair as discreetly as possible.

We stroll into the kitchen, and as the automatic lights kick on, I once again admire the size of it, along with all the amazing appliances it holds.

It's a chef's dream, and I can hardly wait to bake something. Maybe tomorrow I'll ask Irene to show me how to operate the two professional ovens.

"What would you like to drink?" I ask after opening the stainless-steel refrigerator. One side alone of this ginormous box could hold a few people upright.

"A water is fine."

I giggle. "I'm surprised you're not wanting alcohol after what happened tonight."

"I don't drink. Not ever."

"Oh. Can I ask why?" Grabbing a bowl of strawberries, too, I turn around from the fridge with water bottles for the both of us.

I'm surprised to find him staring right at me as he leans back against the massive grey island. His hands are gripping the edge of it, and I have to take a step back from the sight of him.

Gulping, I swallow the saliva flooding my mouth. His naked upper body ... the large bulge in his sweats...

I can hear it over the intercom now.

We need a mop please on aisle Ellis for Camilla's drool.

He's yet another masterpiece in this house to marvel over in the bright light. I have no other words. He lifts his eyebrows and reaches his hand out for the water.

"Sorry. Why is it again you don't drink?"

He smirks. "I haven't answered you yet."

"Oh, right."

"It's simple. I want to be in control of my actions at all times. There are things I know from my job that I can never in my life repeat, and if I got my hands on a computer while under the influence, there's no telling the destruction I could cause. Unfortunately, I learned the hard way that alcohol affects me differently than most people."

My chest tightens, feeling as if it missed a beat. I clear my throat and set the bowl of strawberries on the island, nudging them in his direction before I turn and walk away.

"Is there something in the pantry you'd like? It's Liam's new favorite place," I say as I open the door to it.

"Grab the graham crackers, marshmallows and chocolate bars."

I snicker, and it's a nice distraction from the heavy shit pressing on my chest. After I bring back all the items he asked for, he pulls a long fork out of a drawer and grabs a plate.

Breaking apart the graham crackers, he then lines them up next to each other. Once he breaks a candy bar into squares and sets them atop the crackers, I realize he's making s'mores.

Since he's taking control, I hop up on the island to watch. His gaze shifts to my thighs, and I remember I'm only in thin pajama shorts and an oversized sweatshirt, so I pull on my shirt, covering my legs some with it.

"Don't. I like seeing your legs." Taking it upon himself to push my sweatshirt back to its original revealing position, he then winks at me and struts toward the stove.

"Now, the only safety hazard I need to inform you of is to never touch your mouth to the fork with the intention of biting off the cooked marshmallow. Especially when Irene isn't here to provide first aid. Trust me, I know firsthand."

Looking back, he grants me a dazzling smile, and I must say that I prefer nighttime Ellis over the brooding daytime version.

"OK, I'll keep that in mind." While he turns on the gas burner, I pick out a strawberry from the bowl. "Thank you again for tonight. I know Liam needs to be in his own bed, but it's hard to let go. He's growing up on me way too fast. And he wanted no part of it when *I* tried to read a book to him."

"It only worked with me because the kid was terrified." Ellis lets out a brief laugh, so I shush him.

"Quiet, or he'll be down here eating your s'mores. And you can't fool me; I could hear you being sweet and him laughing in return."

"Don't get used to it. It was a novelty move for me, too."

"Whatever. He likes you now, so you'll never have peace again."

"He's a special kid." Ellis returns with a cooked marshmallow. "Is it done enough for you? Or are you one of those who want it to look like tar before you eat it?"

"Medium brown is perfect. I have a feeling you do this often." He shrugs, so I poke his shoulder. "Someone has a sweet tooth." Upon finishing the assembly of my s'more, he hands it to me.

"Yes, I like sweets. I also enjoy seeing you smile, and I think this is the first time I can take credit for it."

"I'm happy right now."

"So am I." Shifting his back to me again, he goes to the stove to toast another marshmallow. I gawk at his firm ass, the tight shape evident beneath his sweats.

I love this casual look on him. His long feet are even bare, and his light brown hair is sticking up a touch in the back. He's normally so dignified and put together, so I like how he's comfortable around me tonight without wearing a suit and tie.

Ellis returns with his cooked marshmallow, and we talk about Liam for a while. Finishing my s'more, I lick my sticky fingers.

"I make Liam award ribbons when he learns new skills. I'm going to make you a ribbon that reads 'the s'mores maker champion.'"

Stepping between my legs, he takes hold of my hand. My stomach flutters from how close he is and from how his eyes are eating me up.

"You know what else I'm great at?" he asks.

"What's that?"

"Licking and sucking, and I don't think you should just take my word for it." Inserting one of my fingers in his mouth, he gradually drags his lips up it, sucking it, too, as his eyes stare at mine the entire way. With no fight in me, I allow my legs to come up and wrap around his hips.

"You *are* really good at sucking."

"So are you," he says. "You have chocolate on your mouth." Holding the sides of my head, he sweeps his tongue along my lips and swirls the tip at the corner of my mouth, wiping away the leftover chocolate. "I think I need to show you my licking skills next."

"Yes, I think you should."

He smirks. "Camilla Rose, are you actually agreeing with me?" The heat creeps up my cheeks, and I smile.

"I guess I am."

"I think I need to see if you're still a dirty little liar." He grins, letting me know he's being playful and not an asshole.

"I might still be dirty, but I'm not lying."

"Fuck, you're sexy." Letting his head fall against mine, he navigates one hand up under the back of my sweatshirt while the other slips inside my shorts and grabs my ass. A little moan escapes from my lips, so he squeezes harder.

With urgency, he yanks my sweatshirt over my head, exposing my bare chest. He ducks and pulls on my nipple with his teeth, causing me to cry out from the sting.

He's rougher the next time, inciting a pain more than a sting, but I don't want him to stop. For the first time in my life, I *need* so much more sexually.

He sucks on the other nipple while he plays with the first, flicking and pinching it. My temperature's rising, heart is pounding, and I'm trapped by an immense yearning for him. He has to free me from it. He has to this time.

Stepping back, he goes for my shorts, so I lift my hips from the counter. He pulls them off, along with my thong, and grabbing my body, he turns me and lays me lengthwise on the island.

Dizzy with desire, I breathe in deep, inhaling the scent of the chocolate and strawberries next to me. In a heartbeat, he has both of my knees up and my pussy at the edge. As soon as his fingers touch my flesh, I buck.

"You're not lying this time. You do want proof of how good I lick." He shoves two fingers inside me. "So wet, and you haven't even had my tongue yet. You're going to come fast. I sense it."

"Please, Ellis. Please make me come this time."

"It wasn't supposed to happen like this. Us here in the kitchen. You unrestrained and begging already, but I can't resist. You're too damn sweet and tempting."

Securing my ankles with his hands, he leans over and covers my pussy with his mouth. The heat alone spreads like a vine across my skin.

He tongue fucks me next, the pleasure instantaneous and building, so I grab hold of his hair as he shows me just how good he is at licking my clit. He sucks on the hood of it until I can't take the sensation a second longer and pull away.

"Don't think about going anywhere. I'm only getting started with you. Once you come on my face, I'm fucking you rough right here on this island."

Bent over and holding my ankles, his sculpted back and broad shoulders fan out like an eagle's wings, and it's mesmerizing.

His tongue begins a full-fledged assault, stroking down my pussy and twirling wildly along my clit. He reaches up and squeezes my breast, massaging it and tugging on my nipple, over and over again.

"Ellis, I'm going to come."

Thrusting two fingers in me, he continues to lick as he pumps them in and out. The pleasure pummels me to my core, and it's like a sheet of stained glass, shattering as I come. It showers color everywhere I can see, and I'm soon blinded by its intensity and the ecstasy of sensations.

My eyes open, and Ellis is climbing onto the island. He's completely naked now, holding himself up by his defined biceps. The man is captivating.

"Scoot back a little." It takes all my strength to rise to my elbows and move myself farther back on the counter.

"We don't have a condom," I say, panting.

"You're not on birth control?"

"No."

"Well, you know what those fucking stairs are like. I'm not going to get one when I'm dying this second to fill you to the hilt." While still on his knees, he clenches my hips, lifts my pelvis and slams into me before I can reply.

Our backs arch, and I'm in awe watching his shoulders bunch and the veins in his neck pop. His jaw squares off, and I squeeze around his cock that has filled me so full.

"Fuck, yes," he says as he pulls back and thrusts into me again. His movements are powerful, shoving me against the counter of the island repeatedly. Every stroke along my slick center provides further pleasure, and I'm climbing toward another orgasm.

"Your pussy feels incredible." He pounds into me, and the way my pelvis is tilted, allows his cock to rake along my upper wall until I'm overrun by paralyzing sensations yet again.

I unravel and contract around him for the longest time from the most intense orgasm of my life. He groans and stills, coming deep inside of me, and although this definitely constitutes fucking, it feels so intimate without a condom. What was he thinking?

Ellis

I can tell I'm squishing Camilla with my body on the island, but I can't move. Not yet. It's been a while since I've been inside a woman, and never has my cock been inside one without a condom. It feels unreal.

This wasn't supposed to happen. I'm playing with fire, and I don't understand why. My original plan was to whip her into submission. She would be obedient while I make all the rules and use her to fulfill my needs.

Yet here I am, sharing this intimate moment with her after making her fucking s'mores. Not to mention, I read a bedtime story to Liam about a damn poky puppy. Things have quickly gone awry.

I pull my dead weight up by lifting myself with my hands. I'm now over top of her, staring down. Her hazel eyes tilt up at me, and she's fucking gorgeous. Too gorgeous. Blessed with a natural beauty few woman are lucky enough to possess.

Every part of her is emitting a fiery glow I'm drawn to, from her auburn hair, to her flushed skin and rosy lips. Her eyelashes flutter, and she grins.

"I gave you sex, so can we hire Emma?" Biting down on her lip, she smothers a laugh, and I can't believe she's finding humor in the terms she must abide by.

She's sweet and strong ... and I'm fucked.

"I think I'm the one who gave it to you, but yes, we can hire Emma."

Her eyes round, and her grin broadens.

"Really? Oh, thank you. I believe she'll be wonderful to Liam. I have a good feeling about her, and it's hard for me to trust people."

"We should get some sleep." Climbing off the island, I pull on my sweats and help her off. As if embarrassed, she dresses in a hurry, pulling her old sweatshirt over her head. I bought her plenty of clothes, so I don't know why she's still wearing some of her old ones.

"Um, I really need to use the bathroom," she says before she leaves the kitchen.

While she's gone, I clean up the food mess we made, and not wanting to explain to Irene why the island needs sanitizing, I find some all-purpose cleaning spray and wipe it down myself. When I turn around, Camilla is back, but the flush to her skin hasn't faded.

"I've never had sex in a kitchen before." That damn grin is back on her pretty face, and reality of what transpired between us sinks in. She's too comfortable.

"Go to bed, Camilla. I imagine Liam will have you up early." My tone is cold as I turn my back on her to return the cleaner to a cabinet.

"Well, thank you agai—"

"I said go to bed," I snap without turning around. After a few seconds, I shift to face her but only catch a glimpse of her hair before she's out of my sight completely.

She'll be hurt and angry now, but it's necessary. She was already trying to manipulate the situation, asking about hiring Emma right after sex.

From what I uncovered about her past, Camilla's a survivor. She adapts to new situations and environments well, shaping them into what will make her feel safe again, but only one of us can possess power at a time, and it'll never be her.

CHAPTER TEN

Ellis

Hungry for lunch and needing to stretch my legs, I forego having Irene bring me something to eat in my office, and I instead walk to the kitchen.

Admittedly, I'm also curious as to how Camilla will interact with me today after what transpired last night. I've heard little noise in the house, and Christopher hasn't popped in much.

I avoided asking him about her this morning. I didn't want to encourage him to speak with her. I could swear there's a protective look in his eyes when her name is spoken by either of us, and it displeases me. If he's lusting after her, we've got a serious problem.

Reaching the kitchen, I see Irene moving about. After turning to me, she brushes her hands over her apron and sweeps her dark hair from her cheek.

"Ah, Mr. Burke. I was about to bring you lunch. I got a little off schedule since I'm serving Ms. Rose and her son, as well, but I'll make adjustments so it won't happen again."

"It's no problem. Where are they?"

"They've already eaten, so I'm unsure."

"And Mr. Day?"

"I believe he's in the library working."

"Thank you. I'll have lunch in the dining room." Leaving her alone, I stride to the library on the main level and find

Christopher working at his desk. This has become his office until we turn another room into one.

"Hello," I say.

"Hello. I was about to look for you. A Mr. Lawrence made an appointment for tomorrow. He said it's for a personal job, not his business. I saw your calendar was clear at 4:00 p.m., so I added him."

"Yes, I know Mr. Lawrence. That's fine."

"Also, Camilla and Liam are in his room. I believe she's resting on his bed."

"Why would she be lying down?"

"She said she has a problem with her back, and it's bothering her today. I offered to help with Liam, but she declined."

Her back... Our sex last night.

"The nanny starts tomorrow, so we won't need your help with Liam. I'm going to go have lunch. We can talk later." Irritated that he knows more about Camilla than I do, I march out and head to the dining room.

Salmon atop a salad is waiting for me at the table, along with a plate of fruit, but Irene knows to bring me something sweet to eat later. Most of the males in the Burke family prefer scotch, whereas I have a weakness for sweets.

Sitting in silence, I remember why I usually eat my meals at my desk. It's a distraction from the otherwise lonely existence in this spacious home.

Camilla's back is likely hurting because of how I pounded into her on the solid kitchen island, and I can't deny that I'd do it all over again. My cock twitches from the memory alone.

The thought of needing her well and not pissed at me when I take her to the playroom gives me an idea. Pulling my phone from the pocket of my khakis, I Google the nearest flower shop.

"Hello, I'd like to place a delivery."

"Yes, sir," a woman replies. "What would you like to order?"

"I need five dozen red roses."

Once I place the order, I march back to the library to speak to Christopher. "I need you to do something for me."

"What's that?"

"Go to the nearest drugstore, and ask the pharmacist to show you everything over-the-counter that could help ease Camilla's back pain. Pills, a heating pad... Whatever he recommends, buy it."

I start to leave the room but stop and turn. "Oh, and bring the items to my office. I want to be the one who gives them to Camilla." Staring me down, a jealousy from him I previously thought might be a figment of my imagination is confirmed.

"Is there a problem?"

"She was sad again this morning. I don't believe this is where she wants to be, and I've been thinking that maybe it'd be less of a headache for you and intrusion on your space, if you allowed her and her son to return home in exchange for a set visitation with Liam."

I give him a smug look. "It sounds as if you've put a lot of thought into this, which means you've put a lot of time into thinking about Camilla. I suggest you stop that. She's my responsibility, not yours."

Turning my back on him, I grip the doorframe. "Don't worry, I plan to take good care of her, along with my nephew."

Leaving Christopher with that remark to stew over, I march upstairs. I'm about to enter my office when I hear Liam playing down at the other end of the hallway. For some reason, curiosity maybe, I'm drawn that direction. Arriving at his closed door, I listen in.

"Vroom, vroom," he says. "Momma, the car goes super-fast." Not hearing Camilla respond, I crack the door open.

She's asleep on Liam's bed while he plays on the floor next to her. He looks to me with a serious stare, so I smile at the kid. He softens and returns a smile.

"Hi, Boss," he says, and I laugh. Yes, Camilla's going to hate that. She opens her eyes, and upon seeing me, she sits up in bed. Wincing, she grabs her lower back.

"I hear you're not feeling well."

"I'm fine."

"Liam, would you like to see my office?"

He hesitates, but being a curious one like his uncle, he nods.

"I think he should stay with me. I can't have you sending him mixed signals about wanting to spend time with him." She's curt with her words, and I know what she's implying.

"He's going with me, and you better get used to us spending time together. I have three years to make up for, and it's what Tony would've wanted."

Rolling her eyes, Camilla utters something unintelligible under her breath. I'm adding another tally to her list of offenses.

I reach my hand out to Liam, and he looks to his mother for approval. It takes effort on her part, but she eventually smiles and nods.

"You can go. I'll be right here when you get back." She glances to me. "Not long please; he needs a nap."

"And I need you well, so rest while we're gone."

Taking hold of Liam's hand, I walk him beside me down the long hallway to my office.

Once we're inside, his eyes take in all the surroundings, from my massive cherry desk and bookcases to the different trinkets sitting around.

Distinguished leather chairs are to his right with a small table between them. "Do you want to sit in the chair?" He shakes his head no. "Do you wish to sit at my big desk?"

With eyes gleaming, he nods and heads right for it. I help him onto the chair, and his small arms sit atop the leather armrests. Pushing my laptop back out of his reach, I then scoot him close to my desk.

His eyes roam over the space before zooming in on a photo of Tony and me when we were about five or six. I'm only ten months older than my brother, thanks to an affair my father had, so we look similar in age and size.

Liam's blue eyes light up as he points at me in the photo with one hand and pats his chest with the other.

"That's me, Liam."

"Uh, no, that's me."

His forehead scrunches. "That's not me?"

"No, that's Boss."

He snickers and points to Tony.

"Who's that?" Damn, what do I tell him? Camilla and I need to have this discussion.

"That's my brother."

Patting his chest again, his head shakes.

"I don't have a brother."

"No, you don't. Would you like to draw?"

"Crayons?" he asks.

"No, the crayons are in your bedroom. I have pens and paper. Why don't you draw over at that table while I do some work?"

Reaching for my printer, I steal some paper off the tray and grab a few different color ink pens from my desk drawer. I then help Liam out of my office chair and lead him over to the small table.

In a flash, he drops to his knees and begins drawing with one of the pens. As soon as he sees the green ink, he beams up at me.

"It's gween, Boss."

"It sure is," I reply with a chuckle. I tousle his hair and stroll back to my desk. I got this under control. As long as I'm comfortable around Liam, my parents will buy that he's mine. Now, I have to get Camilla on board with the plan.

Camilla

Lying alone in Liam's room, I lift my cell phone and type a long text to Sasha. Then, I remember Ellis is likely spying, so I decide to call her instead.

"Hello," she says before giggling.

"Sasha..."

"Sis, how's it going?"

"OK. How are you?"

"Good. Rusty and I are watching a hilarious movie." She giggles again.

"Sasha, are you high?"

"No, but god, you're such a buzzkill. We're just having some beers."

"I called to make sure you're doing OK."

"I'm good. Rusty's keeping me entertained."

"I'm sure he is." Christopher steps in the doorway and looks around. "Sis, I have to go. I'll call tomorrow."

"OK, love you."

"Love you, too." Ending the call, I sit back up in bed.

"Where's Liam?" he asks.

"With Ellis in his office."

Furrowing his brow, he looks up and down the hallway before stepping inside the room and shutting the door.

"What are you doing? We can't be in here alone."

"I just need a minute with you since we can't text. Why did you let Ellis take him?"

"I didn't have a choice. He genuinely seems interested in getting to know Liam. He even helped me get him to sleep last night."

Chris is wearing a scowl as he comes closer.

"I don't like it."

"Well, it's better than him treating my child like shit or ignoring him completely, which would be confusing to Liam, seeing how we're living in Ellis's house."

He grips his hips and gives me a scrutinizing look.

"You're taking up for him."

"I'm doing no such thing. I'm being amicable for the welfare of my child. There's a difference. You need to go before he comes back."

"OK, but I want more time alone with you so we can work on a plan to get you out of here. Ellis has an appointment at four tomorrow. We'll talk then."

"I can't. I have a doctor's appointment."

"For your back?"

"No, it's something else."

"I'll take you."

"I'm driving myself, and since Emma starts work tomorrow, I'm taking her with me to watch Liam."

"I'm starting to think you don't need me here at all." His hand slides over his short raven hair.

"That's not true, and you know it. I'll call you tomorrow if I get a chance. Now go."

CHAPTER ELEVEN

Camilla

Finally getting Liam down for a nap, I head back to my room. Of course, Ellis kept him in his office for far too long since he thinks he can do whatever the hell he wants.

I'm still angry at him over how he treated me last night in the kitchen. Everything was going great, and I was even finding myself liking him, but then he turned back into the cold man he was prior to his charade, blowing my good mood all to hell.

Entering my bedroom, my eyes spot the crystal vase of bright red roses on my dresser. I walk over and notice the other items sitting next to them.

There's a heating pad, some topical pain patches to place on my back and several medications. Christopher is going to get us in trouble if he doesn't stop this shit. How am I ever going to explain the flowers to Ellis?

There's a knock on my door, so I spin around and stand in front of the roses.

"Uh, who is it?"

"It's Ellis. Can I come in?"

"OK."

"Good, you saw the things I purchased for you. I thought they might help your back until your doctor's appointment tomorrow."

"What appointment?"

"I made you an appointment with my physician. He's going to examine your back for you."

"What time? I managed to get a cancellation appointment with my gynecologist tomorrow afternoon so I can get on the pill."

"It's at two. Will that work?"

"Yes, it should. My appointment is at three-thirty."

"OK, I'll make sure my driver, Fletcher, knows he'll be taking you."

"I was going to drive myself."

"No. That car of yours is a death trap, and I have a driver so he can do just that—drive us around."

"You think I'm going to run when I have the chance."

"That's not why I don't want you going alone."

"I won't run away, Ellis. I wouldn't risk losing Liam. I'll stay here as long as you make me." Remembering the flowers, I look back at them over my shoulder. "Did you buy me the flowers, too?"

"Yes, and there are more in your study and throughout the house." His forehead creases. "Who did you think they were from?"

"Um, I didn't know. I'm just surprised they're from you since you were hateful to me last night."

Strolling over, he clasps my chin and tilts it so I'll look at him. His gaze is sincere, like the one I was lucky enough to see last night.

"I'm sorry. I didn't want you to get the wrong idea."

"What would that be?"

"You manipulated me to hire Emma. Don't think for a second it's going to happen again."

"If you believe I had sex with you so you'd hire her, that wasn't the case." I look away. "I had sex with you because I wanted to. I liked seeing you sweet and playful."

Still holding my chin, he slides his other hand around my waist and brings me closer.

"That isn't the norm for me. I got caught up in the moment; however, I've come to believe it will be more satisfying for the both of us if you submit to me willingly, rather than under duress."

I shake my head. "I don't want to participate in BDSM, or whatever you call it. I'm sure I wouldn't like it."

"How do you know if you've never tried it?"

"I'm not a fan of pain, and after some negative experiences in my life, I have to be in control. I told you that."

His thumb skims over my bottom lip, and his eyes bore into mine with a thick haze of desire. Already, he's imagining our time together, fantasizing about what he'll do to me.

"You need to trust me. I promise I'll bring you pleasure."

"Then you—and please don't get upset when I say this—need to be less hot and cold. You have to show me it's safe to trust you. Threatening that I'll lose my child is not the way to earn it."

His forehead wrinkles, and he puffs out a breath.

"Fine. I'll work on it." Releasing my chin, he presses his fingers into the back of my neck, weakening my knees on the spot. Ever so slowly, he plants his warm lips on mine.

The zing I feel is instantaneous as my body recalls what he did to it only hours ago. It's anticipating more, the electricity between us a jolt to my nerve endings, but I quickly discover this kiss is different.

It's slow and teasing, lips brushing along mine from right to left, and back again ... and back again, and god, back again.

"Ellis, I'm scared you're going to destroy me," I whisper against his lips.

"I won't. I only need the power to." Sensing my weakness, he holds me closer and feathers again a taste of hair-raising pleasure to my lips.

Although it's petal-soft in touch, the electric current is Morse code for a secret longing between us. The message travels straight to my pussy, signaling it to clench in search of his hard cock.

I whimper, the craving overpowering, and I wish I didn't need his touch to feel this alive, but I do. I'm desperate for more, so I open my mouth, encouraging his tongue to slip right in. It moves on cue and at the same taunting pace.

Having to touch him, I shove my hands between us and up into his hair. His low groan fills my mouth as his fingers that are pressing against my neck begin massaging it. The tip of his tongue explores mine, and I finger the coarse strands of his hair while we move in a hypnotic rhythm.

It's as if we're apologizing for the ugly moments shared between us since we met, but knowing I'm still here against my will, can we truly start over?

Separating our lips, Ellis cradles my cheeks.

"The way I just kissed you is how I'm going to taste your pussy tomorrow night. Languid strokes and faint licks to your clit until you're coming apart against my mouth.

"The only difference this time is you'll be bound. You won't be able to stop me, and that's what I need, Camilla. I don't understand why, but I *have* to dominate you. I've known since I stared into your eyes that first night we met."

Once again, the guilt from years ago rears its ugly head, and I know what I have to do.

"OK. Whatever you need, I'll try it," I murmur.

Camilla

Inhaling all the air my lungs will allow, I crack open the door to one of Tony's spare bedrooms. Ellis Burke sits up from the bed immediately and slides a hand over his thick brown hair.

"Can I help you?" he asks.

"Oh, sorry. I didn't know anyone was in here. I was looking for a place to hide out. Care if I join you?" I hold up the bottle of champagne and my flute glass. "I have alcohol."

"I was actually looking to get away from the crowd."

"It's only me, and I promise I won't try to give you a lap dance like the rest of them." I display a timid, sweet smile, hoping he'll take the bait.

"OK, sure." Strolling over to him, I sense his heavy gaze lingering over my scarcely clothed body. The only light shining through is from the cracked door of the adjoining bathroom, but once I'm close enough, I can't miss how attractive he is.

Tony is a beautiful man, with symmetrical facial features and silky hair, but Ellis's characteristics are rugged and pronounced. He has an intimidating presence that has stolen my breath.

His jawbones square off sharply at each side of a cleft chin. He's taller than his brother, more muscular, too. And his deep-set eyes give off a haunting vibe.

Gathering my wits, I pour the champagne in my flute and hold the bottle out toward him.

"Drink up. It might calm your nerves. I don't like big crowds, either," I say.

"I don't normally drink, but I have to admit it's helped this evening. I'm already a touch lightheaded." Laughing, he swipes the bottle from me and holds it to his mouth to take a drink.

He's in jeans, and the sleeves of his burgundy button-up shirt are rolled up his forearms.

"May I?" I ask as I point to the spot next to him. He nods, so I sit. Being on a bed with him while I'm wearing only a short negligee and panties feels intimate.

And wrong.

My god, I've been having sex with his brother.

Of course, Ellis Burke doesn't know that. What feels worse is that Tony put this plan into motion.

Swallowing a drink, I turn to Ellis and smile.

"This is much better ... the quiet. I'm more of a homebody myself."

"Me, too." After taking another drink from the bottle, he turns to me and stares. "I didn't see you at the party. I would've noticed you; you're beautiful."

"Thank you. I arrived late." Although his eyes are glazed over, they're a stunning blue, and I can't help but stare at them.

Becoming more nervous, I drink the rest of the champagne from my flute. He wasn't supposed to be gazing at me in return, acting interested, but he is.

"Let me pour you more to drink, and then we can get to know each other better," he says seductively.

***

"Please get off of me."

His lips kiss up my neck, and I smell a citrus scent from his coarse hair that's tickling my face.

"Let me touch you," he whispers.

"You weren't supposed to do this."

"But you feel so good beneath me. Please, whoever you are, give me this one night with you."

Shoving my arms out in front of me, I spring upright in bed. "Ellis! Ellis!" My eyes fly open, and once my mind registers it was a dream, I cover my pounding heart with my hand.

The beginning ... the end. The dream is always in fragments, and maybe it's better I don't remember it all.

My bedroom door flies open, and the sound of thumping footsteps coming toward me causes me to scoot back farther in my bed. My heels dig in the mattress until my back is pressed against the headboard. "Who's there?" I ask.

"It's Ellis. Are you OK? I heard you yelling my name."

"Please go." The bed sinks in, and seeing his eyes transports me right back to my vivid dream.

"I'm not leaving. What happened?"

"I had a bad dream. I'm fine."

He grabs my hand and presses it between his, but then he touches my forehead and cheek.

114

"You're clammy and shaking." Before I can stop him, he's next to me in bed and pulling me to his side. The only clothes I feel against me are his boxers.

He can't comfort me. It's confusing, and I need away from him. God, I need away.

"Ellis, please go back to bed."

"Don't be embarrassed. I have bad dreams, too. You'd think we would outgrow that shit as adults. Maybe you had it because you're sleeping somewhere new."

Pulling on my body again, he shifts me until my torso is on his broad chest. His lips press to my hair. "I'll stay here with you."

"Liam and I have disrupted your sleep enough already."

"Maybe it was too quiet in this big house before you came."

"Maybe you were also lonely." Feeling his lips press to my head again, I realize I'm safe. He won't hurt me and even came in here to comfort me.

I touch his chest with my lips in a few different spots and feel his heartbeat accelerate. My body moves down his, my lips soon tracing his rippled abs. His fingers delve in my hair, and his fingertips massage my scalp.

"Mmm ..." I hum from the relaxing feel of it.

Hooking my fingers around his boxers, I inch them down until his hardness springs free and is smooth beneath my palm. Twirling my tongue around the head, I taste his pre-cum before I seal my mouth over his length and suck.

Groaning, he spreads open his legs a little, and his fingers clench my hair. He likes it, so I continue to move my mouth, picking up speed.

"Oh, keep sucking, just like that," he breathes.

I do until he tenses and comes in my mouth. What's this man doing to me? Days ago I thought I hated him, and now I'm voluntarily giving him a blowjob.

It's because deep down I've always suspected he's not the enemy. I didn't want to see it because it made his brother and me the villains.

What if what Tony told me about Ellis was a lie? If so, then I was a victim, too.

CHAPTER TWELVE

Ellis

Yawning, I open my eyes and see Camilla's body blanketing me. It's funny how she's sprawled out across me, sleeping peacefully.

Her body's sizzling atop mine, and I can't resist fingering her soft hair. Feeling my cock harden, I sigh and slide out from under her.

Shit, it's eight-thirty in the morning. I glance to the video baby monitor on her dresser, and surprisingly, Liam is still asleep.

He stayed in his bed last night after our agreement that I'd read him a story each time he succeeded. Since he's three, I'm shocked he's held up his end of the deal.

I smile. Like his mom, the kid's cute. Quietly, I shut Camilla's door behind me. I turn and spot Christopher coming down the hallway, but he freezes about twenty feet away. He looks to her bedroom, then at me. Fuck.

At first, he glowers, but then he clears his throat and walks the remainder of distance toward me.

"Good morning," he says crisply.

"You're usually here at nine. Why are you early? Actually, where were you headed, seeing how my office is the other direction?"

"I thought I should get an early start since it will be hectic around here today. I, uh, was going to make sure Camilla was awake since Emma will be here at nine."

"Camilla and I will be down soon. You can go back to your office."

"Of course."

He marches away, his irritation evident in his quick stride. I forgot all about Emma starting today, so I go back inside Camilla's room to wake her.

***

"Thank you for lunch, Irene," Camilla says after she, Emma and Liam walk into the kitchen from the dining room. I'm pouring myself a third cup of coffee at the counter. Having a lot of work to catch up on, I ate lunch in my office.

"Yes, thank you. It was delicious," Emma adds. I look over as she pushes her black glasses up her nose, her short hair matching them.

The doorbell rings, and since Irene's hands are in a soapy sink of water, I tell her I'll get it.

I stride to the door and open it, and shit, it's my cousin Greyson.

"Hi," I say. "What are you doing here?"

"What do you mean what am I doing here? We have racquetball in thirty minutes."

"Oh, right. I forgot. If you want to wait in your car, I'll be out in a few minutes."

He smirks. "You're not going to let me inside?" There's a tug on my pant leg, so I look down.

"Boss, who's that?" Liam asks. "Shit," I mutter before I lift my gaze to meet Greyson's.

His eyes widen, and his smirk morphs into a grin.

"Now, I'm coming in for sure. Who's the kid?"

Puffing out a breath, I step aside and let him in.

"Liam, come with me," Emma says before she takes his hand and leads him away.

"Uh, it's a long story."

"And the woman?"

Camilla steps into the foyer now, looking for Liam.

"Holy shit, two women. This keeps getting better."

Camilla is stock-still, staring at him as Emma walks Liam up the stairs. It's obvious Camilla doesn't know whether she should leave or introduce herself.

"Greyson, this is Camilla. Camilla, this is my cousin Greyson. I forgot we had racquetball, so we'll be leaving soon."

Stepping closer, Camilla stretches her hand out for him to shake.

"Nice to meet you," she says.

"It's my pleasure, and how do you know Ellis?" he asks her, being his nosy self.

"Oh, I'm Liam's mother. Ellis is his—"

"Father," I blurt out. "I'm Liam's father." Their eyes widen in shock.

"Ellis," Camilla utters.

"He might as well know now. He's family, and we have to tell them at some point. Why don't you go up to Liam's room? We should keep an eye on Emma since it's only her first day."

She stares at me, frozen in her spot. "Camilla, go. We'll talk later," I say assertively.

She struggles to slide her gaze back to Greyson.

"Again, it was nice meeting you." Turning on her heels, she stomps toward the stairs. Damn, I'll have to explain this, and it couldn't be on a worse day since I'm introducing her to the guest house tonight.

Looking back at my cousin, I watch him swallow and scratch at the back of his blond hair. He's still wearing his grin like it's superglued to his smug face.

"You have a *child*?"

"It's a long story. One I'll tell you in the car. Let me go change."

Camilla

What in the hell just happened? Why would Ellis want to say he's Liam's father? Oh, the man has some explaining to do.

No sooner than I start to enter Liam's room, Ellis takes hold of my arm and pulls me aside.

"I'll explain later."

I jerk free from his hold. "What were you thinking starting a lie like that?"

"I told you I'll explain later. I have a good reason, so don't stew over it all day."

He's staring at me with sincerity and a touch of worry.

"Fine. I won't."

"Good. You and I are having dinner together this evening, and then I have something to show you."

"But what about Liam?"

"Beatrice will be here. I hired them both. Emma will work days, like we agreed, and Beatrice will be here late evenings and some overnights. There are times you and I won't be in the house, so someone has to be here to watch him."

"Where are we going?"

"I'll show you tonight."

"You're full of secrets today."

"That I am. I'll see you later."

Ellis

I'm riding with Greyson in his silver Rolls-Royce Wraith. Our family comes from old money, but we all work hard to make new.

Greyson's an attorney, but he also invests in real estate, particularly commercial development, and it has paid off well for him.

"Do you honestly think I'm going to let you sit quietly over there?" he asks.

"All right, here's the story; Tony introduced me to Camilla several years back. We had sex, parted ways, and she wasn't sure who the father was. Then, she showed up at Tony's visitation, and we reconnected. After talking, we realized Liam might be mine."

"So, you're not sure."

"Well, I'm pretty sure. Did you not see the kid? He straight up looks like a Burke. He could pass as yours."

He chuckles. "No, he looks like you, not me. Light brown hair, blue eyes ... besides, I'm not stupid enough to fuck a chick without a condom."

"Don't call me stupid. It was a heat of the moment kind of thing."

"You were probably drinking. We both know you're a pussy when it comes to holding your liquor."

I punch him hard in the bicep, and he pulls his arm in toward himself. "Ow, shit. OK, I deserved that. Well, what's with the women being in your home?"

"Emma is the nanny, and Camilla and I are ... dating. She and Liam are living with me, and we're trying to make it work."

"Damn, so you really like this woman."

"Yes."

"I can't believe you didn't confide in me when you found out. I thought we shared everything, man, and had I known about this before you moved their asses in, I would've advised that you get a paternity test first. You should still do that before things get serious."

I consider what he said. I never thought to question whether Liam was Tony's child. I assumed Camilla was sure since she showed up at the funeral home with the photo, and of course, because he looked like my family.

Maybe it's something I should do before I set up Liam's trust fund from Tony's estate. My brother couldn't have hated me too much since he left me as the sole beneficiary.

The thought of Liam possibly not being Tony's disturbs me. I don't want Camilla to have a reason to leave.

***

"How is your back today?" I ask Camilla. She's across from me as we share a candlelit dinner at the dining room table. She doesn't look up and is using her fork to play with the food on her plate.

"It's much better today, but the doctor insisted on running some tests." Her eyes meet mine. "I panicked since I didn't have insurance any longer, but I was told by the office clerk not to worry about the bill. I'm guessing you had something to do with that?"

"I forced you to leave your job, so I'm paying your medical bills."

"Oh, and I really need to use my own vehicle. I didn't appreciate having to cancel my appointment to get my birth control pills all because Fletcher had to be somewhere else for you."

"Uh, yes, I'm sorry about that." To change the subject, I point toward her plate with my fork. "You haven't eaten much of your dinner."

"I'm nervous about what we're doing later, and I'm wondering when you're going to explain to me why you want your family to believe Liam is yours."

"I apologize for today. I had planned to discuss it with you first, but then Greyson showed up, and I was put on the spot." I sigh. "My father cheated on my mother soon after I was born. Tony was conceived from that affair.

"The woman was an escort and refused an abortion, so my father put her up in a luxury apartment. He provided medical care throughout her pregnancy until Tony was born. He then paid her to give up custody, and my mother raised Tony as her own.

"Even after the unspeakable betrayal my mother endured, she chose to stay married to him, and I can't help but think she did that for me. For that reason, I can't bring myself to tell her my father now has a blood-related grandchild."

"It's sweet you want your mother to believe Liam's her biological grandson, but it's still a big commitment to make for only that reason."

"When you have my family's degree of wealth, bloodlines mean everything. My mother deserves this, but if you give me a valid reason why it's important for them to know he's Tony's child, I might change my mind."

"What will we tell Liam if everyone else believes he's your son?"

I look down at the table. "I haven't thought that through yet, but we have a little time."

"Are you also wanting to do this to spare Tony's reputation? Because if so, it's going to tarnish yours, and I don't believe he would've done the same for you."

Dropping my fork, I cross my arms.

"We need to talk about the elephant that's always in the room. What did my brother tell you about me? And I want the truth."

Laying her fork down, she sits back in her chair.

"This is all so confusing. You want to get back at me for not telling Tony about Liam. I know you do, but you're struggling to follow through. And as much as I should want to hurt you for making Liam and me live here, I can't bring myself to try.

"If I tell you what your brother said about you, it will hurt you, especially if it's false, so can we save that conversation for another day? So much has happened in only a short amount of time. You can't deny that. I mean, it's been a whirlwind."

Camilla has a grace and kindness to her that's unmatched by any other woman I've met. I'm beginning to wonder if she had good reason for keeping Liam from Tony. I can't see her being so callous otherwise.

Wiping my mouth with my cloth napkin, I scoot away from the table and stroll around it. I hold out my hand for her to take.

"We can wait to discuss my brother. There's something more important to attend to ... a place I want to show you."

CHAPTER THIRTEEN

Camilla

Lust flickers in Ellis's eyes as his hand reaches out for me. He's handsome as always in a pair of dark jeans and a thin black sweater. Placing my hand in his, I stand and gaze up at him.

"Here's the deal," he says. "Since Liam doesn't know Beatrice well, I'm going to have us do what I have planned now before it gets too late.

"She has my number, so if there are any problems at all, she can reach me. We'll come back inside in an hour or so to put Liam to bed. I already promised to read him a bedtime story."

He smiles, and the way his eyes display happiness when he speaks of his nephew does something to my heart. This man is an enigma I can't stay away from.

"OK, and thank you for thinking of him." As we leave the dining room and reenter the grand hall, I hear the TV in the family room where Liam is watching a movie with Beatrice.

It's difficult to resist stopping in there to give him a kiss, but I'm trying to learn to coddle him less.

"Wait here," Ellis says before striding away. As always, I stand in awe in the amazing space. The staircase we take every day is across from me, and the sun is setting through the windows behind it, casting an orange glow over the magnificent room.

Ellis strolls back with a black trench coat and hands it to me. "Go to your room, and undress until you're nude. Put on a pair of heels, and return in only this coat."

"Are we going out in public?"

"No. Now, do as I said. I want plenty of time with your nakedness."

His words open the gate for my nerves. They scurry beneath my skin, multiplying as the word spreads about the party we're about to attend. Not wanting to appear eager, I delay running up the stairs until I'm out of his sight.

Once undressed, I go to my closet and find black heels that match the coat. Thankfully, I have a few pairs from working at Octavia. I cinch the belt around my waist and head back downstairs, taking each slick step carefully.

A faint smile edges from his lips as he eyes me. He takes my hand and leads me toward the back of the home until the sound of the television has faded away. We stop at two glass doors, and turning back to me, Ellis cups my cheeks.

"We're going to my guest house. It's a playroom, but you can think of it more like our little hideaway, where I can do with you as I please."

"Is that why there were workers back there? Were they getting it ready?"

"Yes. Ever since I told you the terms."

"You've known for that long what you were going to do with me?"

"Yes, and I've fantasized about it every day since, especially after having a sampling of you. Now, once we step out this door, don't question me. You do as I say. Understood?"

"Yes, Sir." *Where the hell did that come from? Yes, Sir?*

He swallows hard, and it's satisfying to see I have an effect on him, too. Gripping my hand, he leads me into the cool air and onto the patio. Since I'm seeing it for the first time, I survey the area.

There's a fireplace encased in stone and plenty of outdoor furniture. What looks like a bar is set up, too, and I wonder if Ellis even uses this space since he's not someone I envision hosting a party.

Once we're off the patio, we walk along a sidewalk to the guest house that's tucked away to the left, about one hundred feet behind the main home.

He pulls a set of keys from his pocket, and as he sticks one in the lock, I lose my breath and fear my heart might beat out of my chest. The feeling reminds me of the first time I danced at Octavia.

He steps inside and pulls me behind him. A light is switched on, and I'm surprised when I see a small kitchen and a dinette set to my left. There are stainless steel appliances, like in the main home, and the counters are a sleek black.

Beyond the kitchen is a living room with a black leather sectional that is covered in red and grey pillows. A glass table sits in front of it, and there's a large television hanging on the wall.

Still clutching my hand between his, he brings it up and kisses it.

"Come on. There's more to see." He starts down a hallway and points to the first door on the right. "Spare bedroom."

Straight across from that room is another door, and Ellis pushes it open. Stepping inside, I'm first surprised by the size of it, especially the length. It stretches far back, maybe forty feet to the right.

I look to my left and eye a wall of hanging contraptions. I can identify several of the items from having worked at Octavia.

Many of the dancers at the club engaged in BDSM with our clients off-site, so they would often tell stories and show me things on their phones when I was curious as to what they were speaking of.

I can't say I haven't been intrigued, but never have I thought it's something I would enjoy. That is, until Ellis blindfolded me.

I never dreamed I'd like it, but I did. My senses were beyond heightened, and I can still recall how his cock felt in my hands and mouth.

"What are you thinking about?" he asks.

Strolling over to the wall, my fingers glide over a flogger.

"How your cock felt in my hands and tasted in my mouth the day you blindfolded me in my study."

My arm is grabbed, and I'm spun around. Yanking me to him, Ellis smothers my mouth with a kiss. A hand fists my hair while the other squeezes my ass through the coat.

Groaning, he comes up for air and pierces me with a look of anger, something I wasn't expecting.

"You're to relinquish control in this room, not try to gain it."

"I was only answering your question honestly. I'm sorry." My gaze drops to the floor as I feel shame for disappointing him.

He unties my coat and peels it over my shoulders, letting it fall to the floor. I begin to tremble, feeling cold, as well, but I resist the urge to cross my arms.

"Your body is sensational, but there's something I want you to wear over it." Walking away, he goes to a dresser at the right where we came in.

While I wait, I view the room before me. I'm standing on a shiny black floor, and most everything in the room is either black, grey or red.

Crimson roses are in glass vases on two dressers and a nightstand by the bed. Picking up a black velvet box, Ellis strolls over to me.

"This is a gift, and you will wear it every time we're in this room." Taking it from him, I steal a glimpse at his eyes, trying to gauge his mood. He doesn't seem angry now, but tonight he's serious Ellis.

Popping open the long box, I cover my chest with my hand as I discover a stunning necklace. A pear-shaped ruby is dangling below a sparkling round diamond. It drops from a platinum chain and is exquisite.

"It's beautiful ... Sir." I lift my eyes again, and although he doesn't speak, the appreciation is evident in his gaze. I've yet to figure out all the reasons I want to please him, but I can't stop myself from making the effort.

"Turn, and I'll put it on you." Doing as he instructs, I pivot and hold up my long hair. As soon as it's clasped, I can't resist touching it at my chest. "Let me see."

I turn back, and his eyes fall to it. He's staring keenly, and I wish I knew his thoughts. "It was made for you," he utters. "Let me show you around."

With my hand in his, he leads me farther into the room. About midway, black metal framework, which is slotted and a couple of feet wide, runs across the ceiling and down each wall to my right and left.

"What will you do with that?" I ask while pointing.

"I'll tie items to it that I can then tie to you."

I nod, unsure of what my head thinks while my hand wants to give a fist bump. The pulsing between my legs, which I so often feel around Ellis, has returned full-strength.

Walking ahead, I admire the king-size bed that's centered to my left. It's adorned with a black duvet and silver pillows.

A full-length leaning mirror, also in silver, is propped against the wall across from the bed. It's intricately designed, giving the sensual room an elegant feel.

"That door there is a bathroom, and the one to the left is a walk-in closet you'll soon be familiar with. Aside from today, when you come in this room you are to wear something from that closet. You get to choose, but right now I want you naked."

Lacing our fingers, he walks us to the bed. There's something about the way he joined our hands that makes me feel safer. It's as if he's letting me know we're doing this together.

Once we're at the side of the bed, he gives me a soft kiss. It's faint, and as his lips brush back and forth across mine, I remember what he promised to do to me tonight.

Releasing my hand, he folds back the duvet and top sheet. "Climb up, and lie on your back."

Once I'm positioned on the center of the mattress, I wait impatiently as Ellis strolls to a dresser by the mirror across from me. He returns and tosses grey rope next to my leg.

With his gaze boring into mine, he begins stripping his clothes at the foot of the bed. His loafers are toed off, socks removed next, and the front of his hair sticks up in a sexy, haphazard way after he takes off his black sweater.

Folding it, he sets it on a bench at his feet and then removes his jeans and boxer briefs. He's taking his time, attempting to taunt me, and it's working.

Coming around to the side of me, he picks up some of the rope. "Hands above your head." I raise them, and he pins my wrists together before he ties them to two spindles on the headboard.

I look up and watch him form an elaborate knot I can't get out of. My heartbeat races, and my breaths become quicker, too.

"I'm nervous," I whisper.

His lips skim over my ear before his breath fills it.

"Don't be. I'm going to make you come hard and more than once. Pick a safe word."

Grabbing the last two bunches of rope from the bed, he eyes my legs. "Bend your knees up to your chest. Now, let them fall open but keep them bent."

Placing the rope over my shin, he then wraps it behind my thigh and to the front again before he ties the two ends together. After examining his work, he repeats it on the other leg.

"What's your word going to be?"

"Marshmallow."

He smirks. "We'll discuss the reason for that later."

I'm now bound to where I can't straighten my legs. Feeling exposed more than ever, I jerk on my wrists, but they won't budge.

"Don't shut your thighs. If you do, I will add an extra spanking to the ones you're already receiving tonight."

Crawling across the bed, he aligns himself between my legs. On all fours, he dips his head and brushes his mouth across my stomach. His arms bend so he can move lower, and he drags his tongue once down my pussy.

I start to snap my thighs shut from the tickle of it, but I recall what he said and stop myself. I don't know how many spankings he plans to deliver, or how hard he will hit, so I have no desire to add another one to the count.

Dropping to his forearms, he settles between my legs, and spreading me open, he skims his fingers down my slit before he shoves them in his mouth and drags them back out.

"Mmm ... you're already wet and taste sweet. You might be nervous, but you trust that I'm going to make you feel good."

Getting back to it, he spreads me open more, and almost too faint to feel it, he touches my clit with his tongue. He skims around it before flicking it lightly.

"No, no, no, faster," I say.

"Are you telling me what to do?"

"I'm sorry."

"Sorry, what?"

"I'm sorry, Sir." Applying a little more pressure, he circles my clit again, but as soon as the pleasure begins to rise, he backs off. Getting the urge to grab his hair and push him down so he will lick me harder, I jerk again on my arms.

"I feel like you're resisting me and what I want to do to you."

"No, Sir. I only want more."

"And I want you to relax and let it build gradually. I should've blindfolded you. Close your eyes."

"Yes, Sir." Settling against the bed, I let my eyelids shut. I breathe in and out, focusing only on what he's doing to me.

Envisioning his wet mouth, I imagine how my juices are coating the outside of it. I picture the tip of his tongue tracing my clit, and I can see his pressed fingertips against my pink flesh as they pull me open. I moan, not only imagining but feeling how his tongue pushes inside my tight pussy.

"Yes," I say through a whimper. His tongue darts in and out of me several times before he drags it back up to my clit.

He twirls it around the opening, and the sensations are intensifying, growing with every stroke. My release is imminent as I focus on all the exquisite things his mouth can do.

Without warning, he slides two fingers inside me. He hooks them around toward my front wall and begins pressing against my G-spot.

Lord, he knows what he's doing. The pleasure quadruples in intensity as he pumps his fingers and flicks his tongue at my clit.

"Oh, I'm so close." Moaning, I struggle to find the air to speak. "Please, Sir, may I come?"

"Yes. Come now, my Rose," he says, his voice muffled. He won't let up, pressing my G-spot until it's close to painful. He repeats the same phrase, over and over again, as I revel in my orgasm.

Growling, he releases me. I open my eyes and see him rising to his knees. His mouth is soaked, and his hair is a sexy mess. God, he's so handsome.

His long cock is stiff, and in seconds, he's pressing his palms against my knees and driving my legs toward my chest.

"Condom," I utter.

"No." His lips purse, and I'm stunned silent before he slides his dick inside me. Letting his head fall back, he glides it in and out in a steady motion, and now he's the one doing as he instructed; he's focusing on how this feels, likely imagining my soaked pussy taking in every inch of him.

He pulls out almost all the way before he thrusts hard, and fills me so full. "I love fucking your cunt. Damn, I love it."

Gripping my knees tight, he slams into me, striving for an orgasm.

It's not long before he stills and groans, coming deep inside me. Thank the heavens I took pain meds today. He has no mercy on my body, but I wouldn't have it any other way.

Once he's caught his breath, he unties my legs and wrists. I stretch as he moves to the side of the bed.

"Lie over my lap."

"Right now?"

"What did I say about questioning me?" Without responding, I drop my gaze and step off the bed. I can't believe I'm voluntarily giving my ass up for a spanking. I think his hard fucks shook my brain loose.

Standing next to his legs, I gnaw on my lip and stare down at the bead of cum still on the tip of his cock. Since I'm not moving, he takes it upon himself to flip me over his lap.

I can't help but squeal, so he places his hand over my mouth while bracing the back of my thighs with the other.

"I'll gag you if you're not quiet. If you cry out while I spank you, I will add another one."

I nod, and he removes his hand from my mouth. Placing it over my upper back, he then swats my ass. I buck from the sting of it, so he braces me tighter.

He strikes me again, across both my cheeks, and only a few seconds pass before he repeats it. "I've lost count of the times you've challenged me since we met, so I'm going to go easy on you and spank you only ten times."

He continues, and each strike is more intense than the last. Tears well up in my eyes from the blood rushing to my head and from the sting to my ass.

The confusion of it all is leaving me emotional, too. I'm in pain, yet I like giving him this control, ultimately pleasing him, and it reminds me of when I tried to please another man close to him. I was determined to do it no matter the cost, and I was left devastated. Will Ellis break me that way, too?

I cry out on the ninth hit, feeling the burn. "Did you think I was bluffing? Now you get eleven." He massages my cheeks before landing the final two blows. I taste blood once he's finished, and I realize I've bitten into my lip.

As he massages my ass, he strokes my back. His fingers move up into my hair, and he plays with it, relaxing me a bit. The next thing I feel are his fingers pushing inside me.

It takes only seconds before I shove my ass up, yearning for more of the pleasure. The sudden intrusion of his finger inside my mouth startles me. "Suck," he orders. I do, and he groans before pulling it free from my lips and sliding it between my ass cheeks.

I wobble a bit on his lap, so he opens his legs some to balance me better. Swirling the tip of his finger around my asshole, he groans again. "I can't wait to fill this tight hole with my cock. Have you ever been fucked there before?"

"No, Sir." I moan from the pleasure of his fingers working over my pussy while his others play with my asshole. He inserts a fingertip, and it's my undoing.

"Baby, come now."

I orgasm, and I think my head could explode from being tilted over.

"Come on my fingers, my Rose. One day soon, you're going to orgasm on command by hearing only those words."

My body quivers, and I'm completely under his power. He's controlling my body, possibly my mind, and what's terrifying is how he's affecting my heart.

His fingers slip from me, and he stands me up. As he watches, I pull the hair away from my wet face, and upon Ellis seeing my tears, he wipes them from my cheeks, furrowing his brow in the process.

Without uttering a word, he lifts me and lays me back on the bed. His body covers mine, and with his cock hard again, he sheaths himself inside me. There's no barrier between us, and although it's risky, I can't deny it feels sensational.

Wrapping his hand around my wrists, he pins them above my head and rocks his scorching naked body against mine. He palms my breast and massages it as his tongue eases between my lips.

It explores and strokes gingerly, and having him take my body this way, so deliberately, causes it to tremble. It's as if he planned the entire scene and wants someone watching to witness this final show of ownership.

His lips trail down my neck and to my chest before his smoldering mouth suckles my nipple, his movements slow and direct. Holy shit, the buildup of this sex is like nothing I've experienced.

His hardness ebbs and flows inside my pussy, never picking up speed, until all at once, his fingers clamp tighter around my wrists. I float in euphoria as our orgasms collide, and through it all, his lips stay pressed to my burning skin.

He's done it.

I submitted.

He claimed me.

Ellis Burke's wish to possess my mind, body and soul is coming true.

CHAPTER FOURTEEN

Camilla

Waking up early, I lie in my bed and stare at the baby monitor. Liam is sleeping, and I reflect on watching Ellis last night as he read him a bedtime story.

I wonder if Ellis considered that I could be spying on them. It was a beautiful sight, but it was also odd to see him flip that switch and be gentler than the man I'd been with only minutes before in the guest house.

My experience with him was like nothing I could have imagined. My preconceived notion was that I'd suffer through it, but the evening ended up amazing, and I'm different today because of it, feeling more desirable.

Coveted ... that's the word, but in a way that gives me strength.

How can I find this submission acceptable after being forced to live here? Can I be a true submissive to him if I'm being held against my will?

Questions like this are what kept me up most of the night. What I do know is there is a good side to Ellis Burke. I feel it and see it.

Needing to find out what the day will bring, I head to the bathroom and get ready. I showered last night after being with Ellis, but I hop in again for a quick one.

Once I put my hair up in a loose bun and apply makeup, I roam into the walk-in closet and look around. All the storage units are white, and there's plenty of overhead lighting in the room.

To the left is a long hanging rack, and multiple dressers are past that. Straight back is a full-length mirror, and on the right side of the closet are cubbies for shoes and handbags.

It's unreal how nice the space is, and it's strange to have an abundance of clothing to choose from. Gracie at Octavia would have a field day in here.

After I've picked out a delicate lace bra and panty set, I pick up a cream sweater and run my fingers over it. This has to be cashmere. I look for the tag and discover I was correct.

Once it's on, I notice the scoop neck is low-cut, revealing my cleavage. I pull on some dark boot-cut jeans and a pair of short boots to match.

Seeing how it's late February, and the temperatures will be milder soon, I want to take advantage of wearing boots before it's too late.

Stepping in front of the mirror, I admire myself, and I'm amazed how much better this outfit conforms to my figure compared to my old clothes. I can't deny that I'm pleased with how I look today.

Strolling back in my room, I see on the monitor that Liam is sitting on his floor, stacking his Lego blocks. My mouth falls open in surprise over how comfortable he seems, playing in his room alone. He's happy here.

It's quiet in the hallway as I walk to his room. I open the door, and his face lights up.

"Look, I have lots of these blocks," he says.

"Good morning, and I see. You're such a big boy playing in here by yourself. Let's go to the bathroom and get you dressed."

"I went to potty aweady."

"You did? All by yourself?"

"Yeah, Boss gave me my own bafroom."

"You keep saying that name. Who's Boss?"

"That tall man who reads me books."

"Oh, really? Did he tell you to call him that?" Having lost interest in me already, Liam barely nods and goes back to playing with his toys.

Arrogant Ellis. I think that's a good nickname for him.

I find some clothes in Liam's closet and give him no choice but to dress and head downstairs for breakfast.

Christopher is pouring himself a cup of coffee in the kitchen. He barely glances my way but then does a double take. His green eyes rake down my body before he shakes his head and goes back to what he was doing.

"Good morning," I say.

"Morning," he mumbles before he strides out of the room without even saying hello to Liam. It dawns on me that he avoided me yesterday, too.

"Good morning, Irene."

"Good morning, Camilla. What would you and Liam like for breakfast this morning?"

"Emma won't be here for another half hour, so could you fix Liam some oatmeal and help him with it at the table? I need to speak to Mr. Day."

"Absolutely." She takes Liam's hand. "Good morning, my piccolo. Would you like some blueberries in your oatmeal this morning?"

I leave them alone and stroll to the library Christopher's using for his office. Like my study, it's lined with bookshelves. There are polished leather chairs and side tables, and his desk sits to the right of the room. The morning sun is filtering in between the thick damask drapes.

"Hi, can we talk a minute?" I ask.

"No, your *boyfriend* will have an issue with it."

"What?" I look in the hallway again, and not seeing anyone, I shut the door behind me. "If Ellis shows, I'm here to tell you the books to order for me. Now, what's wrong?"

Planting his elbows on the desk, Christopher threads his fingers and narrows his gaze.

"I saw him leave your room yesterday morning, Camilla."

Shit. I rub my earlobe. "I had a bad dream. He heard me yelling and came in to check on me. I was pretty upset, so he stayed with me and fell asleep."

"So you're telling me he didn't fuck you?"

"Don't *ever* speak to me like that again. No, I just told you what happened."

He sighs. "I'm sorry. It was surprising to see him come out of your room, especially when you just got here and he doesn't know you."

"Look, he's not hurting me, so you can ease up on the worrying. He's being good to Liam and me."

His eyes squint again. "You like him."

"Stop putting words in my mouth."

"Answer me honestly, Cammy. Are you starting to like him?"

"Fine, yes, he's not so bad." I look away, knowing how terrible this seems.

"I can't fucking believe this. You don't like me after all the years I've been there for you, but after only a few days around Ellis Burke, who mind you is holding you hostage by way of blackmail, you already like the man. Do I need to remind you that you had his brother's baby? It's like watching a bad soap opera unfold."

"Screw. You. Get off your high horse, and don't speak to me until you can do it with respect."

I storm from the room and back to the kitchen. Asshole. I don't want to think about what he said. Is it wrong for me to be with Ellis after having Tony's child? Ellis doesn't seem to mind. This situation is messed up, and I'm mostly angry because I know what I have to do.

Ellis

It's 8:45 a.m., and I'm refreshed as I trot down the stairs to the kitchen. Having experienced the best night of sleep I can recall in years has me in a great mood this morning.

I even had the dreaded dream about the woman in red, but this time, I could see the shape of her eyes, not just the color of her irises, and they were Camilla's.

My plan is working. I'll continue to gain power from her submission until the bizarre, unsettling dream stops resurfacing.

Stepping into the kitchen, I spot the tray Irene has prepared to bring up to my office. There's a water pitcher and glass, my vitamins, a muffin, and an empty spot that's no doubt for my mug of coffee.

She probably wonders why I keep coming downstairs, but I now have a reason to. There are people for me to see, and I hear the laughter from them drifting in from the dining room now.

"Mr. Burke, I was about to come up. Can I pour you a cup of coffee?" Irene asks with a smile. Even her mood seems brighter today as a light surrounds her dark eyes. I believe she enjoys having Camilla and Liam here, too.

"Yes, a cup would be great. Three sugars today please." Once she hands me my mug, I stroll to the dining room.

Camilla's back is to me, and Liam's legs are swinging beneath his seat at the head of the table. He's talking fast, and

I'm only understanding every few words. Spotting me, his eyes brighten.

"Boss, hi."

Camilla doesn't turn around, but I can't miss the way her shoulders lift as she sucks in a breath.

"Good morning, Bob. How are you?" Flinging his head back, Liam covers his mouth and snickers.

"My name's not Bob."

"Oh, right, it's Carl."

"Noooo, it's Liam, but you can call me Mikey."

"Mikey? Where did you come up with that name?"

"*Ninja Turtles*," Camilla utters, still not turning around. I lean down and put my mouth to her ear.

"Good morning, my Rose." Her breath hitches, and I believe she snapped her legs shut.

"Morning."

"You're in my spot, *Mikey*," I say to him as I walk behind his chair and sit across from Camilla. "Where's Emma?"

"She should be here any second. Can we talk after?"

"Sure." I'd like to do more than talk to her now that I've seen how beautiful she is today. The swell of her magnificent tits is visible in her tight sweater, and her bare neck is calling to be kissed or even better—bitten.

"Good morning," Emma says cheerfully after stepping into the dining room. Leaning over and smiling at Liam, she pushes her glasses up her nose. "What kind of trouble are we going to get into today?"

"I'm not in trouble."

147

"Yes, let's avoid trouble," Camilla says.

"Are you finished with breakfast?" Emma asks him.

"Yep."

"Then let's go upstairs. I have some cool games in my bag we can play that will make us smarter. You want to get even smarter, don't you?"

He sports a grin as Camilla attempts to pull his face in her direction to wipe dried oatmeal from the corner of his mouth.

He can't get out of his chair fast enough, eager to take Emma's hand, and it's good to see him comfortable with her this early on.

The young woman is eccentric with her black painted fingernails that match her dark hair, glasses and makeup. Along with a loud yellow sweater and purple jeans, she's wearing Converse tennis shoes that look like they're covered in a comic book scene.

Interesting, but as long as Camilla and Liam are happy and she cares for him properly, I'll live with her quirkiness.

"Let's go to my office to talk."

Camilla's chewing on her lip and looking around the dining room. She's nervous, but not in the way I'd like her to be. Whatever's on her mind is weighing heavily.

"Don't you want to eat your breakfast?" she asks.

"Coffee will do for now."

Only nodding, Camilla leads the way to the stairs, and that's fine by me since it gives me a chance to stare at her incredible ass as we climb them.

Once we're in my office, she turns back to me, clasps her hands in front of her and lifts her chin.

"I have something to say."

I smile. "I gathered that, and I think you conjured up some confidence with each of those steps we took, whereas my cock twitched more with each of them after staring at your ass, so please make it quick so I can touch you."

Her finger comes out to wag. "Yes, see, we definitely need to have this discussion now."

Sighing, I take a drink of my coffee and stroll around my desk to sit down.

"You seemed content last night when we returned from the guest house."

"I was. Last night was amazing."

Pleased, I smile. "Then what's the problem?"

"I'm not going to have babies by two brothers. I mean, what does that say about me? And we're just getting to know each other. It's strange to me that you're willing to be so careless."

Crossing her arms, she raises her eyebrows. "So, I'm insisting we use condoms until I get on birth control, which I intend to do at my appointment I rescheduled."

"OK, fine."

"Oh, well, then good."

"You seem surprised by my response."

"I am ... and there's something else. Something much more important."

"What is that?"

"I can't be your submissive if I'm being held against my will. I was up most of the night, mulling over this situation, and for it to work, I have to trust you."

"And I told you I would work on what you requested"–I wave my hand in the air–"about me being hot and cold or whatever the hell it was. I thought I was doing much better."

"You have been, but it doesn't change that if I leave here, you'll demand Liam stay. I can't accept that and be who you want me to be. A Dom and sub's relationship needs to have a foundation of trust."

Oddly, she begins walking backward until she's against my closed door. With her arms still crossed, she leans her head back against it and looks to the ceiling.

"The experience in the playroom confirmed how intimate our relationship will be both physically and emotionally, at least for me, and much more so than engaging in sex on a kitchen island."

My heart is racing, my irritability rising as I sense where this is headed.

"Get to the point, Camilla. What the hell are you wanting?" I snap. White-knuckling the arms of my chair, I inhale slowly, attempting to calm my anxiety.

"Respect, Ellis. Self-respect and respect from you. What kind of mother am I if I allow you to treat Liam and me like possessions?" Stepping forward enough to reach behind her, she opens my door.

"If you want me to be your submissive, to give myself over to you completely, then you're going to have to tell me I'm free to leave if I ever wish.

"I don't know if what Tony told me about you is true, that you do dangerous, sketchy work, but regardless, I don't believe you'd ever harm Liam.

"What I'm trying to say is I'd never keep him from you if I did leave, but if you want our physical relationship to continue, you have to give me this. You have to give me the freedom to go."

On her final word, she slips through my doorway, the space now void–seeming empty of the breaths the house was beginning to take. What the fuck?

CHAPTER FIFTEEN

Ellis

Instead of Dean, I'm the one tapping out, and it happens in only a short round of mat work. He lets me go, and more out of embarrassment than anything, I stay on my back and stare at the recessed lights above.

"Man, where's your head at today?"

"I should've cancelled. I thought I needed the outlet, but you're right that my head's somewhere else."

"Is this about your brother, or does it have more to do with the attractive woman you introduced me to?"

"Tony dying is still fresh, of course, but Camilla's fucking with my head, too."

With a grin, he holds his hand out to help me up.

"I'm on the clock for thirty more minutes, so why don't you fill me in."

"Asshole." I shake my head and hop up without his help. Grabbing a towel off the shelf, I wipe the back of my neck. "Want a water?" I ask him as I reach in the mini-fridge.

"Sure." After grabbing us both one, we have a seat on a bench at the side of the gym.

"I can't say much about it, but I have to do something I don't want to do if I stand a shot with her."

"That's with every relationship, man."

"Yes, well, I don't know shit about being in a relationship. Basically, she wants me to be less controlling. I have to set her free with the hope that she fucking stays."

"OK. I can't imagine what that's really about, but maybe you need to think outside of the dojo to resolve this issue."

"What do you mean?"

"Often we focus too heavily on one technique, one move, to get our opponent to submit, so if that's not working in your life, or with this chick, maybe it's time to try something different. If it's comfortable and easy to get what we want, then maybe we didn't earn it or deserve it."

"Damn. That may have earned you the title of sensei."

"Take it as advice from a friend with experience. I almost lost Meredith before we were married because I was holding on too tightly. Instead of watching me act like a caveman, she needed to see I trusted her."

Dean's words are thought-provoking, but what he doesn't know is that I stacked all the cards against myself when I started this arrangement with Camilla.

I was just beginning to knock them down when she confronted me with this ultimatum. Can I trust that she won't leave if I do ease up on the reins?

Camilla

"Damn, this car is sweet," Sasha says as she glides her fingers along the seat next to where she's sitting on the passenger side of the Mercedes E-Class Wagon I'm driving. "Do you think he's giving you this car?"

"Like I said, I don't know. Christopher only told me that Ellis purchased it and insisted I drive it." I roll my eyes. "Mr. Burke believes my car is a death trap."

"Well, can I have that death trap? I could really use some wheels."

"We'll see. With everything up in the air, I might end up back at the apartment." Propping my elbow on the door, I lean my head against the window.

"Momma, when we be at the park?" Liam asks from the backseat.

"Soon, sweetie. Only a few more minutes."

"How long do you think Ellis will go without speaking to you," my sister asks. What's up with her? She's never this nosy about my life.

"I don't know, Sasha. It's been three days, so surely soon. Christopher is loving it, though, having to be the go-between."

"Oh, yes, I forgot about the love triangle."

"Will you stop? It's not a *love* triangle at all. That would require me feeling love for some part of this 180° cluster fuck."

"Oh, look at you, Smarty Pants," she replies.

"Moooomma, you said a bad word. A *verwy* bad word." Catching a glimpse of him in the rearview mirror, I spot his stern expression and scrunch my nose.

"You're right, Liam, and Momma's sorry. We don't use that word."

"How does he even know that's a bad word?" Sasha asks.

I shoot her a sideways glance. "You're kidding, right? I'm sure you get the credit for that one."

"Boss says that bad word, and he puts monies in my piggy bank every time. I got *a lot* of monies in there."

Sasha giggles first, and I can't help but join in, and then ... I can't help but cry. The buildup of tears tumble fast and heavy, a snowball, picking up speed, except this one is warm and salty, full of disappointment and a bottomless sadness I can't explain.

"Momma? You OK?" Liam asks. His sweet, concerned voice envelops me like a baby blanket to soothe my hurting heart. I look back at him, and he's straining his head, eager to see my face. Swiping my tears away, I suck up my emotions.

"I'm fine, and look, there's the park. Are you ready to play?" Thankfully, his attention span is all of three seconds, so his mind is now in the fun zone as I pull into a parking spot on this beautiful Sunday.

"I've got him," Sasha mutters before hopping out of the car. I use the time to find a tissue in my purse and collect myself.

Ellis and I barely know each other, so why does it hurt so much that he isn't speaking to me? If I'm honest, it's because my mind was beginning to imagine the possibility of a future with him, and for some incomprehensible reason, he saw it, too.

Hell, he pushed me that direction, and fast, but it was a stranglehold, and what can be built from that?

Remembering I came here to enjoy time with my sister and son, I exit the brand new vehicle and stroll over to where Sasha is helping Liam climb a small slide.

"Momma, watch me do it all by myself." The midday sun gifts me the twinkle in his blue eyes and the sparkle to his teeth as he grins. All at once, I *really* notice it. I see how much he resembles a Burke. I see ... Ellis, and I fight back the tears all over again.

***

"He's sound asleep back there," Sasha says after twisting in her seat to check on him. I pull up in front of my old apartment, and after searching around in my purse, I withdraw an envelope and hand it to her.

"I already paid next month's rent, and I'm paying the utilities online. You should be covered, but here's some grocery and spending money."

Handing it to her, I keep a hold of one end. "Promise me you'll find a job soon. There's enough extra in here to buy yourself a nice outfit to wear to interviews."

"I promise, and thank you for the money and for lunch today."

"If I find out I'm staying at Ellis's, then I'll give you my car to drive, but I can take you to work in the meantime."

"I promise to look this week."

Releasing the envelope, I manage a weak smile.

"I'm worried about you," she says. "You're falling for him, and I don't want to see him hurt you the way Tony did. It was messed up what that man did to you."

"Yes, it was, but I got Liam out of the deal. Don't worry about me. I always find a way to survive, even in the darkest of situations.

"Ellis Burke is difficult, demanding and confusing, but he's also generous and sometimes kind. This situation could've been a hell of a lot worse."

I shrug my shoulders. "He and I are at an impasse, but he's too impatient for something not to happen soon. I'll let you know when I have the answers."

"I don't say it enough, but I love you."

"I love you, too. Now, get out of the car before I cry again. We'll talk soon." I wait to ensure Sasha gets inside the apartment.

Even though she doesn't contribute a dime, I feel guilty leaving her here, especially when I think of what kind of house I get to return to. She was sober today, and that makes me want to give her the world.

Camilla

The afternoon is depressing. Liam and I have been hanging out in the family room for a few hours, and it's about time I heat up leftovers for our dinner.

Rain has moved in, and other than the sound of it tapping on the windows, reminding me of its gloomy presence, the house has been quiet. Irene and Christopher aren't working, and if Ellis left his office any, I haven't heard him.

Not being able to take another minute of cartoons, I shut off the television.

"Liam, do you want to eat dinner and then make cannoli with me?" The newfound excitement of getting sweets brings him to his feet.

"Yes! I wuv cannoli." He hurries ahead of me, knowing exactly where the kitchen is. I search through the pantry and fridge, expecting Irene to have the ingredients stocked, and I'm right.

I barely knew my Italian grandmother, but from the little time we spent together, Irene reminds me of her, both of them sweet and helpful, with a comforting smile.

The last time I saw her was when she came to America to visit. I was eighteen, and it was just before I fled with Sasha, protecting her from our junkie parents. I knew then I'd likely never see my grandmother again, and the disappointment is still raw.

Picking up Liam, I set him on the kitchen counter. He swings his legs and grins.

"Momma, can we make Boss some cannoli, too? I bet he would like them a whole lot."

Hiding my hurt behind a smile, I kiss his rosy cheek that's a little windburned from playing at the park.

"Sure, we'll make him some, too."

Ellis

I'm in my office working, dwelling on how the last three days have been total hell. Besides my session with Dean, I've only gone back and forth between my office and bedroom.

Irene served me my meals upstairs, and since she left at one yesterday, I've barely eaten at all, only going downstairs while Camilla was on her outing today.

I was in a panic while she and Liam were away, wondering if she'd take the opportunity to flee with him, and the most weighted breath escaped me when I saw her on the security camera, pulling back in the driveway.

As soon as I got the shocking news yesterday about Tony's death, I wanted to go to her. First to tell her, then to hold her, and lastly to fuck her, needing to feel like I still held a shred of control.

I know what I have to do, what's the right thing, but I haven't found the courage to do it. I take off my readers and toss them to my desk. I rub my eyes and look to the clock on the wall. Seven-thirty.

I should eat something before I go to Liam's room. Every night, after Camilla puts him to bed, I go in and read him a bedtime story. It's our thing and is a promise I'm not breaking unless I'm given no other choice.

Bypassing the stairs, I walk down the hallway and pause at Liam's room. I hear him and Camilla talking. The door is shut, and I can't help but wonder if she doesn't wish to see me again. Is she done with this whole mess?

I turn back and stroll down to the kitchen. Once inside, I spot a plate of something, and my first thought is that Irene dropped by. I walk over, and next to a plate of cannoli is a note.

Ellis,

Liam wanted to make these for you. They're probably not as delicious as Irene's, but Liam and I do have a little Italian in us, so I think they'll be to your liking.

Underneath her note is Camilla's signature, along with a big letter "L" that I can tell Liam wrote. My hand covers my tightening chest. *Fuck.* I think I love the little guy already.

CHAPTER SIXTEEN

Camilla

In the darkness of my room, I stare at the video baby monitor, watching Ellis read to Liam. The last three nights, when he closed the book and kissed my son on the top of his head, a sadness washed over me. I didn't want to see him disappear out the door, and tonight is no different.

There he goes....

Rolling the opposite direction, away from the screen, I close my eyes with the hope that sleep will take away the racing thoughts about the unanswered questions looming.

My door cracks open, so I roll to my back. I see that it's Ellis from the hall light filtering in. I feel paralyzed, aside from my beating heart, which is hammering faster with each of Ellis's forward steps. He sits down on the side of my bed, and I hear his exhale.

"Camilla..."

"Yes."

"I have my suspicions as to why you fled South Carolina with Sasha over a decade ago. You had grounds to do it, so it's wrong of me to hold that over your head.

"Knowing what my brother was involved in, I suspect you had good reason not to tell him about Liam, as well." I see his shadowy shape hunched over next to me. His elbows are resting on his knees, and he's clutching his hair.

"With that said, if you want to leave my home, I won't stop you, and I won't turn you in for what you did. You should also know that Tony left me his estate.

"I'll turn it over to you for Liam's care, and I'll help any way I can. Just please, if you do choose to go, let me see him regularly. I need Liam in my life, and I believe he needs me, too."

In sync are our strangled swallows. The hammering in my chest has climbed to my ears, and I'm burning up all over.

"I hope you choose to stay," he whispers.

He starts to rise, so I lunge forward and wrap my hand around his wrist, pulling him back down.

"I don't want to go. I only needed to know I could." Scooting forward, closer to him, I find his shoulder and kiss it through his t-shirt. "I want you to stay, too ... right here with me tonight."

That's all it takes for him to pounce on me. He clutches my waist and pushes me back on the bed. Rising to his knees, he yanks off his shirt. My pajama tank is tugged on until we're both pulling it over my head.

Falling on me, he presses his blistering body to mine. He's devouring my mouth, grinding against my pelvis and grabbing me anywhere and everywhere. It's not enough, and I don't know if it could ever be.

He's on his feet next, removing his pajama pants. The bedding is thrown back, and finding my thin shorts, he jerks them off.

Covering my flesh again, he shoves to get between my legs. A hand's on my breast, his lips to my neck. I'm tugging on his hair and dragging my nails down his back. Neither of us can get close enough–fast enough ... deep in each other's skin enough.

"Please, no condom," he utters in my ear. "Let me be this close to you, buried inside you. Fuck, you have to let me."

"OK." One word is all it takes for him to thrust his way in, filling me wholly, but it's still not enough, so I arch against his body, desperate to have him bury his cock farther.

A throaty growl travels from his lips before he latches on to my nipple. He bites down and tugs until I'm moaning from the sting while immersed in that place of ecstasy between pleasure and pain.

As he drives into me, he bites and sucks on my tits, my neck, and my chest, undoubtedly leaving marks everywhere, claiming me once more.

"Come, my Rose. Come now." His lips mouth the words against my flesh, and they're a strike of lightening, sending a current throughout my body.

The buildup of sensations is too much to bear, so I wrap my legs around him, dig my heels into his firm ass and cry out, allowing my body to come, come, come...

Thrashing beneath him, I drown in an abundance of pleasure. His face presses to the curve of my neck, and his groan floods my ear as his cock pulses inside me.

Our orgasms meld, and our bodies share our individual emotions, telling everything we can't yet find the words to say.

Getting our breaths, Ellis rolls off of me and brings me to his chest. His mouth presses to the top of my head.

"Thank you for staying. I don't only need Liam; I need you, too."

"I'm where I want to be." I press my hand to his heart and take pleasure in the feel of its healthy beat.

"Camilla ... my brother was poisoned."

***

Ellis and I are in the family room on the sofa. We're eating cannoli and drinking coffee, which we'll probably regret when our busy day begins tomorrow, but after what he told me, we couldn't stay in bed. *I* couldn't stay in bed. Tony was poisoned to death, and I can't believe it.

My feet are atop Ellis's lap as I stretch out, pressing my back against the arm of the sofa at the opposite end.

"Who, Ellis? Who would do something like this?"

"I don't know. We thought Tony took the pills from the empty bottles found next to him, but those drugs weren't even found in his system. They only discovered cyanide, so his death looked staged.

"It will be hard to narrow down a suspect since my brother dealt with a lot of bad people. We could all be in danger now, so I'm going to have security watching the house, and you can't go anywhere without them." He squeezes my foot and gives me a look of warning. "Promise me, Camilla, you won't."

"OK, but what makes you think Tony was involved with dangerous people?" Ellis sets his coffee on the table in front of us.

"It's time to get the elephant out of the room. What did my brother say about me? I need you to tell me everything."

I break my gaze, and my grip grows tighter around the handle of my mug. I told Ellis I needed to feel I could trust him, yet I'm holding secrets that could make him hate me.

"He said you were the bad kind of hacker. What are they called, black-hat hackers?" His gaze drops now, and I hope it's not out of guilt.

"Then he lied to you. I'm considered a security expert. If you want to get into labels, then I'm considered a white-hat. I do ethical hacking." He smirks. "Well, I stray a little, obviously, considering how I tapped into your information.

"My primary job, though, is to protect critical networks. I do private work for corporations, checking for vulnerabilities that could be breached.

"And don't share with anyone, but I have contracts with multiple government agencies. I help prevent horrible things from happening to this country and around the world."

"No..." I shake my head, about to come unglued. "He portrayed you as the very opposite. He told me he was good, and you were corrupt. Why would he do that?"

Ellis shrugs. "I never understood a lot of the things my brother did. Jealousy maybe. He hated that he was the bastard child. He was still a Burke, but he struggled to see it that way.

"He was always jealous of me, feeling as if I was our father's favorite child since our parents could look at me without shame.

"Or maybe it was greed. We have so much fucking money but it never seemed enough for Tony. He always acted like it would somehow be taken away from him."

I nod, recalling what Christopher told me about Tony worrying I'd take his money.

Ellis leans his head back against the sofa. Running a hand through the front of his hair, he stares off. "He did dishonest shit to acquire more and more wealth. It was what divided us. He wasn't ethical in his career, and I often worried it would ruin my reputation and cost me my contracts."

"He made you out to be evil and dangerous, so when you blackmailed me, I felt all his words were validated. I was terrified for both Liam and me."

Lifting his head, he sighs and gazes at me.

"I'm sorry. What I did to you was wrong. I was angry ... grieving, and at that time, I thought Tony took his own life. I truly believed if he'd known his son, he'd be here today." His hand slides up my lower leg.

"I was also drawn to you, Camilla. When I met you at the funeral home, I felt like I'd known you for years. It sounds ridiculous, but it was as if you were this woman who'd slipped through my fingers, like a first love who got away.

"You were the woman I had to get back." His head shakes. "Damn, I can't believe I'm telling you this, but you're different. I can be open with you in a way I never could with anyone else.

167

"Honestly, you were right that I wanted what Tony once had. I was envious of his ability to charm everyone in a room. The man was fearless, cocky and smooth, whereas I always kept to myself. I'm socially inept." He exhales a clipped laugh.

"It's a fact I can admit, and that makes for difficult situations when your family is in the public eye, hosting social function after social function.

"When you're anti-social like me but have wealth, along with women throwing themselves at you, wanting a piece of the pie, it's uncomfortable to say the least. I'm not unappreciative of my life. I know I have a great one, but it's been one spent alone because of my issues."

How do I tell him what I did now? Would he forgive me for believing his brother?

"Ellis, I'm so sorry. I'm sure Tony loved you. He just had his own issues, too. I imagine it wasn't easy for him to know what his father did to the woman who raised him as her own. I'm sure it was like you said; he was jealous of you."

"I think I'm having this conversation with you because it was one I never got to have with him. One that might've helped our relationship or made a difference in his behavior ... a difference in keeping him alive.

"Baby, this is serious shit. I'm talking about stuff you see in movies. He might've been assassinated for things he knew or was going to do. It's why I have to take precautions to keep you and Liam safe."

"This is a lot to take in." Thinking about how my secret could destroy us, I feel a dire need to be closer to him, so I set my food on the coffee table and move in his direction. Straddling him, I give a soft kiss to his lips.

He squeezes my ass and brings me closer. His mouth engulfs mine, sharing a fervent kiss. It's desperate, full of longing and lust, and one day soon I have to confess to him about knowing Christopher and what Tony made me do, but it can't be tonight. We've been through enough.

CHAPTER SEVENTEEN

Ellis

My parents and I are working today at Tony's home, attempting to sort his belongings for an estate auction. We need to decide what to keep and what to discard. I'm alone in my brother's office, and the room is a disaster.

He wasn't neat like me, and it doesn't help that the detectives rummaged through his things, looking for evidence. Thankfully, they don't know where his safe is hidden. A safe that may hold sensitive information; secrets that could tarnish my family's name.

I've avoided opening it for hours, worried of what I could uncover inside. Since I have to take its contents home to look through, I decide to get it over with. Locking the door to his office, I go to the credenza against the wall.

I shove it over, revealing my brother's safe. We exchanged our passwords years ago, before he was corrupt, in the case something like this happened to one of us.

I put in the code, and *son of a bitch*, he changed it. That conniving shit. Falling to the floor, I sit and think. My brother was smart, but not smarter than me. I can figure this out.

I try several codes from various dates of importance, knowing damn well Tony wouldn't use anything obvious. Not with his job title.

I rub my temples. I'm tired, having stayed up late with Camilla. Meeting her turned my life upside down, mostly in a good way, but it's been stressful nonetheless.

Camilla ... Liam. No, it's not possible. Why did the thought even cross my mind? He didn't know about his son. There's not a reason to try, yet my fingers can't help but punch in my nephew's birthdate.

I hear the click, the unlocking of the truth. I fall back to my ass again and bury my face in my hands.

No. Just fucking no.

I finally get the courage to look inside the dark box built into the wall. There are tons of documents I'll have to go through over time, but I shuffle through the huge stack, looking for something about Liam.

His birthdate is the damn code, so there has to be at least one piece of evidence that substantiates what a heartless dick my brother was, and then I find it.

The words *Camilla Rose* are written on a large white envelope that's closed by little silver clasps. I open it and find pictures of Camilla taken from a distance.

There are a few of her and Liam out in public places and some that appear recent from the looks of Liam's size. Lastly, I find his birth certificate. No father listed.

Tony knew about his child and did nothing to be a part of his life, or Camilla didn't tell me the truth, but I can't see a reason for her to lie.

As soon as she felt threatened in my car that night she would've told me Tony knew. Not to mention, she was living at poverty level. If he was seeing Liam, she would've been in a better place financially.

How could he not take care of his son? How could he be such a selfish bastard? Growling, I stand and look for anything to throw. Spotting a round glass paperweight, I grab it and launch it across the room. It connects with a bookcase, rattling it loudly.

"Ellis, are you OK?" my mother asks as she knocks on the door.

"Just a minute," I yell before I shut the safe and quietly slide the credenza back in place. Blowing out some of my anger, I march to the door and open it.

"What are you doing in here? What was that noise?"

"Something fell off the bookcase. I'm still packing up Tony's things."

With the back of her hand, she dabs at the sweat above her lip. From her bun, blond strands of hair have fallen around her face, so she brushes them back.

Her hair color should be grey, but she's determined not to give in to that fact. She's even in jeans, which is unusual for her. She's almost always dressed impeccably.

"Your father and I are exhausted and taking off for the day. We'll return tomorrow."

"OK."

"Don't forget we have that benefit dinner coming up. This one is of the utmost importance, so I expect you to attend."

I roll my eyes. "Mother, you say that about every event you host."

"This one is in honor of your brother. Remember? You said I could auction off his collection of paintings to raise money for the Burke Literacy Foundation, so I expect you to be there."

"Fine. I'll, uh, need an extra seat at our table."

"Are you bringing a date?" Her voice is an octave higher as she attempts to hide her smile.

"Yes. Actually, she's more than that to me."

"Oh, who is she? I'm sure I know her family." My mother, Estella, is now clasping her hands in front of her as the Ellis movie plays in her head, with herself cast as the main supporting role.

There are scenes with the planning and execution of a grand wedding and a joining of two affluent families. It would showcase the parties, dinners, showers, and whatever else people like her do for attention.

That's not my style, and I guarantee it's not Camilla's, either; although, she'd show grace through anything. I'm sure of it.

"You don't know her family. She's not from this area, and much like me, she keeps to herself. She's into philanthropy, though, so you two should have plenty to discuss."

"Now, I'm really intrigued." Mother grabs me for an embrace. "I'm happy for you and can't wait to meet her."

"I need to get back to work. You get some rest."

After she leaves, I'm plagued with panic. Do I tell Camilla that Tony knew about Liam? Would it crush her to think he cared so little about her and their son? *Their* son.

I can't stand the sound of it since I've developed feelings for her. And after what my brother did, he doesn't deserve to be Liam's father.

What if this news makes Camilla leave? She'd no longer have an obligation to stay, no guilt for believing Tony didn't know.

She'll be bitter and will never want his last name on her child's birth certificate. *My* last name. And I couldn't blame her since right now I'm ashamed to call him my brother.

Camilla

My next quarter of online classes begins tomorrow, so I'm in my study after lunch, getting a head start on reading before our first assignment is posted.

Rubbing my eyes, I yawn. Since Ellis and I were up most of the night talking and having sex, the exhaustion has caught up with me.

Emma is keeping an eye on Liam while he naps, so I think I'll take a short one myself. I have a feeling I'll be dragged to the playroom soon, and there's no way I could keep up with Ellis without sleep. I stroll to my bedroom, pull the curtains closed and get in bed.

"Red's your color," Ellis says as he rubs his fingers along the bottom of my negligee. Fingers that are getting close to my bare thigh and panties. "It matches the auburn in your hair."

"Thank you." I rub my temple. "Damn, the champagne seems stronger than usual."

"Probably because we drank the whole bottle." He holds it up before setting it on the nightstand, along with my glass. He falls back on the bed next. "Lie down with me. We can be dizzy together."

This could lead to trouble, so I hesitate, but if I refuse, he might leave the room and look for Tony. He can't find out his brother left the house to go to his. He'll be suspicious for sure.

I lie back on the bed, my head making the decision for me. It spins and spins. Ohh, I'm lightheaded, so I shut my eyes. Much better...

"You seem easy to talk to. I think it's because you're not asking me how many zeroes are behind my name. Hell, you haven't even asked me my damn name." Ellis's last words are slurred before he laughs.

I suspect his behavior is out of character for him since Tony described his personality as serious and drab. He also said Ellis can't hold his liquor and will pass out within five minutes.

Well, we've surpassed the five minute mark, and I'm becoming anxious. Maybe he'll pass out soon, and I can sneak out.

"So, what is your name, Lady in Red?"

"Let's keep this night a mystery," I mumble as I try to stop the tilt-a-whirl I'm riding on. My hands reach out, but there's nothing there. I feel around to gain my bearings until I suddenly realize I'm patting Ellis's firm stomach.

In a heartbeat, he rolls onto me. My eyes fly open, and he's so close. Ellis Burke is so close and so good-looking, and he smells yummy, too.

"It usually takes me longer to warm up to a woman, but you're sweet and easy to talk to," he says while his eyes open and close ... open and then close. Mine are doing the same.

"Something's wrong. We shouldn't feel like this from a bottle of champagne."

"Maybe something's right. Maybe we're supposed to be right here, right now, sharing this moment together, because I can say with certain—certainly—with absolute certainty that you feel incredible beneath me."

"I want to fall asleep so my head will stop spinning."

"And I want you."

Oh, fuck. "Please get off of me."

His lips kiss up my neck, and I smell a citrus scent from his coarse hair that tickles my face.

"Let me touch you," he whispers.

"You weren't supposed to do this."

"But you feel so good beneath me. Please, whoever you are, give me this one night with you."

Fighting to hold my eyes open, I see the sincerity in his. He presses his lips to the corner of my mouth in the gentlest way. They move up my cheek, and then press to my forehead.

"You're genuine. I feel it," he exhales.

"I guess somewhere inside of me I still am, but I don't know that girl anymore. I had to lock her away years ago and become someone distant and untrusting, all to keep my sister and me safe. It gets lonely."

Why am I sharing my secret with him? It's one I've never told a soul.

"I'm lonely at times, too. Wearing armor and feeling misunderstood. But I don't know what I'm protecting. My heart maybe."

My fingers find his hair and play in it. We stare into each other's eyes, sharing an intimate moment, a telling of secrets.

His lips land on mine, and I can't deny I'm getting aroused. His erection presses between my legs and against my thin panties.

His tongue pushes inside my mouth, and his hand massages my breast. His touch is soft, not threatening, and I realize I've passed the point of control. I want Ellis Burke to touch me. For some reason, I want him to know me.

What's happening? My god, the tilt-a-whirl ride won't end.

His lips swirl over my nipple before he pulls down my negligee and finds the stiff peak with his wet mouth. I moan from the pleasure of him sucking and nipping.

"Fuck, you smell so good, and those sounds... Let me inside you," he breathes against my lips.

"OK."

Sitting straight up, I discover I was dreaming. I'm dressed, and sweating beneath my clothes.

"Oh, my god," I utter.

Moving to the side of the bed, I lean my head back and gasp for air. All these years I figured we passed out before he could do anything. We were drugged, so I assumed he couldn't perform. I mean, we could barely hold our eyes open.

Rubbing my forehead, I struggle to see through the fogginess of that night. Even under the influence, there was this connection between us. An intimacy, like two lost souls found their way home at that precise moment.

I remember it now.

I remember Ellis Burke being inside of me.

My phone buzzes on my nightstand from a text message, so I lean over and grab it.

I need to know your hard limits, my Rose.

Ellis

While working in my office after dinner, I look down at my watch. Five more minutes, and Beatrice will be here. After my discovery at Tony's, I felt my control slipping away more than ever, so I called her and asked if she could sleep over to care for Liam. I knew I had to take Camilla to the playroom.

I need this—she needs this. She was different again this evening, likely stressed over the news that Tony was poisoned, but we're not going backward.

She knows that once Beatrice arrives, she's to go straight to the guest house and change out of her clothes. I'm getting hard just thinking about it.

Actually, I've been battling an erection ever since she sent me a list of hard limits while I was still at my brother's. Yes, I fucking texted her from his house, asking for them, and I hope somehow he knew it.

I loved my brother, but he was an idiot to let someone like Camilla walk away, and I can't begin to comprehend his rationale for not seeing Liam.

I think what hurts more than anything is he didn't tell me about it. His loss, my gain. I'll take care of them better than he ever could.

CHAPTER EIGHTEEN

Camilla

Stunned, I cover my mouth with my hand.

Red.

Red.

Red.

I walk along the closet in the playroom, touching each article of lingerie. Every *red* article of clothing. Oh, no. It hits me like a semi barreling fast. I was wearing red the night we were drugged by Tony.

Does he remember me? Is this a game to him? What if this moment is part of his master plan to destroy me? Maybe he's leading me on, sucking me in so I'll fall for him and get accustomed to this life of luxury, only to take it all away from me, along with Liam.

I sit down on a bench that's another reminder of Ellis's wealth. Its cushiony seat is upholstered a light grey, and it's held up by fancy black legs.

I don't know what to do. If I confront him with accusations, he'll be angry for sure, especially if his heart is in the right place. All our secrets must be shared for us to trust each other, so I have to start somewhere and tell him about Christopher.

I go over to an elegant grey dresser and open it. I find a pair of red thigh-high stockings that are adorned at the top with silky bows.

At least they look nothing like what I wore that first night we met, so if he doesn't remember me, they shouldn't trigger the memory.

I'm pulling on the second one when I hear him in the other room. I freeze and listen to his footsteps as he moves around. Slipping on a pair of spiked black heels, I examine myself in the mirror.

Damn, I could use a boob lift. Having a child did a number on my body, but I guess it could be worse. My hips are wider, too, but the curves don't look so bad.

Nervous as hell, I approach the door, and my hand trembles on the knob. I gradually open it, and Ellis turns to me. While his eyes soak me in, he pinches his lower lip like he so often does.

"Come here," he says authoritatively.

Being careful not to slip on the shiny floor, I walk toward him, admiring him as I go. He's wearing only dark grey sweats, similar to the ones he had on that night in the kitchen, and he's barefoot, too. He's holding the ruby necklace he gifted me.

"Turn." Hooking the clasp at the back of my neck, he then presses his lips to my shoulder, causing the hair to stand up on my arms. I swear I can feel his appreciation as he turns me back to face him. "Kneel."

Doing as he ordered, I kneel at his feet and sit back on my legs.

"Sir, may I please speak?"

"Go ahead." Slipping his fingers under my chin, he lifts it.

"I need to confess something. It's important."

"Does it have to do with our time in the playroom?"

"No, Sir."

"Then you will wait until tomorrow to tell me."

I can't say I'm looking forward to the conversation, so I nod in agreement.

"I'm struggling to know where to begin with you. With so many options in this room, it's hard to choose. Stand again."

Once I'm upright, he takes my hand and leads me over to the left of the bed. A plush raven rug is on the floor, and on top of it is a red cushioned ramp.

It appears foam-filled, and attached to it at the bottom of the short slope is a cushiony wedge to use as a pillow. I can't help but notice, too, that there are restraints on both sides and at each end of the ramp.

"Lie over the ramp on your stomach with your hips resting at the top of it. I'll be right back."

Getting on my knees, I lean over the cushion and rest my forearms on the wedge. I find I'm rather comfortable, but I have an alarming thought of how my ass is in the air, perfectly positioned for Ellis to spank if he wishes.

Sensual music fills the room, and I recognize the artist, Alan Walker. A drawer opens at the dresser, causing my breath to hitch. The wait is enthralling in itself, gripping me to my bones, holding me still for Ellis's return.

I eye his backside and how his sweats hang low on his hips, revealing the top of his ass. So help me, I want to squeeze the firmness of his cheeks.

Strolling back, he then squats next to me and sets some items down beside him. I heave for a breath as he puts my wrist in a black leather cuff and buckles it. He moves around to the other side and does the same. I'm still on my forearms but shackled to the wedge.

He holds something up in front of my face.

"This, my Rose, is a pinwheel." There's a devilish sparkle in his eyes as he holds the metal handle. He rolls the device over his fingers, and I notice the pins sticking out of the wheel are rounded at the tips. Gently, he glides it along my forearm, creating a tingly sensation. "How does that feel?"

"Prickly but good." Setting it down, he holds up another item.

"This is a butt plug. I'll ease it in before I fuck your pussy from behind. Something I've wanted to do since you first gave me attitude in my car."

Holy. Hell.

"Lie down on your chest and relax." Although I'm restrained, I'm able to move my arms enough to rest my cheek on my hands.

Lowering to his knees, about center to my body, he begins moving the pinwheel across my shoulder. I know this because I feel the prickly sensations.

It's not painful like I first expected it to be. There is the faintest sting, and as he glides it over my other shoulder, my body quivers, and I hum from the stimulating motion.

He skims it down the center of my spine, igniting my arousal, especially once he reaches the curve above my ass. It rolls up each side of my back, and I relish in the spine-tingling feel of it all as I get lost in the sensual sound of the music.

I take notice of the lyrics in the song "Faded" that speak of someone disappearing or only ever being imaginary ... a fantasy. I've come to realize how much that night we shared years ago affected Ellis.

The intimate time between us was a contrasting kaleidoscope of light and dark. A colorful confusion, yet a clarity of truth. We were two complete strangers baring our souls amidst a blurry fog.

My closed eyelids can't hold back the forming tears. A couple of them manage to slip from the corners of my eyes. Ellis and I were meant to find one another.

I feel it...

I believe it.

This is genuine.

Ellis

Setting down the pinwheel, I press my lips to the center of Camilla's spine. My fingertips skim down her back at each side, and my cock aches over her moans and her shuddering body.

The way her chest is pressed against the slope of the ramp, so she can inch her ass higher in the air, incites a growl from deep in my chest. I want her so damn bad. To fuck her hard from behind. To own her at this moment.

My tongue darts out, and I drag it down her spine, causing bumps to rise to the surface of her skin. Moving behind her on my knees, I glide my hands along her hips before I pull back on them just a touch, teasing her of what's to come.

Her arms come out from under her cheek, yanking the restraints, the sound like a dinner bell for my cock. I'm so fucking hungry for her.

I spread her ass cheeks apart, and she's on her forearms in an instant, shoving her ass up for me. My tongue skims down her crack until it reaches her slick cunt.

She's soaking wet, her pussy waiting for me to have a taste ... to fuck it with my tongue and my cock, slow at first, and then hard and fast.

"God, yes, Sir. Please give me more," she begs through a moan.

Fucking hell. I want to give her more. My shaft far up her ass is what I'd like to give her. My mouth covers her pussy, and

I eat her out. She's practically dripping on my face as I lick and stroke her, pulling her cheeks apart more.

She's saying the word *Sir* repeatedly with a chorus of moans, and every time she gets to the brink, I ease up. I continue this several times, preventing her orgasm.

"Please, Sir, let me come."

Finally, her wish is my command, so I flick her clit until she breaks into a thousand pieces against my mouth. I hold her hips still to keep her from collapsing.

Fuck, I want to rush along, to get my dick inside her, but at the same time, I never want this to end. I stretch over and grab the lube from the floor.

Squirting it all over her ass, I watch as it shines even up into the two sexy dimples of her lower back. My fingers spread it along her asshole before I pick up the butt plug.

"Baby, breathe as I slide this inside your ass." Her back rises with a deep inhale, and she sticks her ass up farther. I knew she fucking wanted this. Barely inserting the tip, I watch as her muscles clamp around it. "Breathe ... try to relax."

She does it for me, and it allows me to inch the plug into her. Within a minute, I have a few of the four and a half inches inside. Her moans haven't subsided, and I'm about to come from the way her ass twitches as her muscles squeeze the plug tight.

Imagining my cock in its place, I can't take another second, so I shove down my sweats, and holding the butt plug steady, I glide my shaft into her tight pussy.

"Oh, I feel so full with both," she utters.

"That's right. Take us both." I pull back, and pushing the plug completely in at the same time, I sink inside her once again, deeper this time.

"Fuck, you feel sensational." Clutching her hip, I begin moving faster. I'm slapping against her ass as she squeezes my cock, and the sight of her is going to be my undoing.

Restrained wrists.

Her arched back.

Her perfect lubed ass at my service.

Erotic red stockings.

And a plug deep inside her asshole.

Christ. "Come now, my Rose. Come now."

She does as I order like I'm the fucking majesty. My dick couldn't be clenched tighter by her pussy, and as we come together, I slide the plug out from her ass.

She cries from the pleasure, her whole body shaking in ecstasy, and I can't remember a greater moment in my life. "Shit, baby, yes," I manage to say through a long groan.

I drop the plug to the floor, and wrapping my arm around her upper thighs, I fall over her back, wanting to be skin to skin with her. I also feel the need to collapse as I come down from an immense high.

Figuring she's uncomfortable, I reluctantly move and undo her restraints. Helping her down from the ramp, I pick her up and carry her over to the turned-down bed.

With her eyes closed, she scoots over to make room for me. I climb in next, and without hesitation, she moves back to me and presses her feverish body to mine. Her arm circles my waist as we both heave for breaths.

"Thank you, Sir," she whispers.

Kissing her silky hair, I pull her closer.

The woman in my dreams is real, and she's all mine.

CHAPTER NINETEEN

Camilla

Sitting in my chair with my back to my desk, I stare out the window in my study at the sleet coming down from the grey sky. The temperatures in Denver are beginning to rise but not enough for the ice to be rain.

I, however, am the furthest from cold. My body still burns from within as I fantasize over the night spent with Ellis in the guest house. Our hideaway.

I gave up studying since his touch and dominance are all I can think about. I'm working toward a master's in public administration, and Ellis is a distraction I can't afford to have, but hell if I'd stop him. I'm hooked. I never thought I could have an addiction, but he might be it.

I jump from a knock at my door.

"Come in," I say as I swivel around to face my desk. Liam skips in with Emma following behind. She's holding her stomach and is pasty white.

"Emma, are you OK?"

"No. I've been sick since right after lunch."

"Hmm..." I look to Liam. "Sweetie, does your stomach hurt?"

He smiles. "Nope, but Emma threwed up in my bafroom." His forehead scrunches, his smile turning upside down. "It was nasty."

"Well, I don't feel sick, either, and we all ate the same thing for lunch. Maybe you're getting a stomach bug."

"Maybe."

"You should go home. We'll be fine here."

Her head shakes. "But you started classes today. I need to stay."

"No, you shouldn't. Please go home and rest. Liam's due for his nap, so I can get more done then, and besides, I'm sort of distracted today."

"If you're sure, then that's probably for the best." She grips her stomach tighter. "I'd hate for anyone else to get sick."

I follow them out of the room, and once Emma leaves, I put Liam down for a nap.

"Boss didn't read me a story last night." Crossing his arms, he scowls. "Bea isn't funny like Boss."

"Well, Boss was busy last night. Reeeally busy," I mumble.

"What was he doing?"

"Uh, he was playing."

"With trucks like mine? Or my Wegos?"

"Um, no. It was with big-boy toys." I snicker. Geez, this is turning inappropriate. "He'll read to you soon, but right now, would you like Momma to read you a story?"

Smiling from his bed, he pulls the sheet up to his chest. My sweet boy. He's getting attached to Ellis, more so than I could've imagined, and I pray neither of our hearts get broken. The only way I see that being preventable is if Ellis and I continue to open up and trust one another.

Is it possible we could turn what began so ugly into something beautiful? I hope so, but who knows what his response will be when he finds out the truth about Christopher.

Ellis

I stroll inside my home, and the familiarity allows me to breathe. It's depressing at Tony's, and I feel like the only task I accomplished there today was the act of shuffling papers around his desk. I was too distracted by the images of a beautiful, sexy woman.

Camilla and I fell asleep in the guest house last night, but it wasn't until after I exhausted the both of us, which took a while.

I awoke to the smell of coffee and her in a scarlet satin robe. She was smiling brightly next to the bed, holding a mug out for me.

I don't think I could wake up to anything better, and the more days I'm near her, the more I'm certain I want her to stay. Tempted to go see her now, I stop at the top of the stairs and look down the hallway.

I remember she's doing schoolwork, and considering the time, I imagine Liam's asleep in his room. Heading to my office instead, I shut the door and shoot Christopher a text, letting him know I'm home.

I heard him downstairs in his office when I arrived, but I didn't stop to talk since I'm avoiding the discussion I need to have with him about my brother being poisoned.

Christopher's going to be interviewed any day by the detectives, though, so I need to deliver the news soon. I want to be the first to hear if he suspects someone.

Knowing that now is the best time to do it, I leave my office. My eyes widen when I see Liam on the third step of the staircase. Camilla is straight ahead, both of us running toward him from opposite directions.

She yells, and it startles him, so he twists his body back to look at her. His arms begin to swing as he starts to fall backward, so I lunge straight for him.

"Liam, no!"

Camilla

"Liam!" I shout. Ellis loses his footing as he grabs him, and they begin tumbling down the floating, spiral staircase, moving fast and hard. "No!"

The thuds from them bouncing down the stairs are like cracks of thunder to my ears. They come to a stop at the first flat platform before the staircase curves again. They had to have tumbled down a dozen steps.

Screaming at the top of my lungs, I run down the stairs after them. Ellis is on his back, holding Liam to his chest. My son's eyes are full of terror as he stares up at me on his back. He bursts into a blood-curdling cry as the realization of what happened hits him.

Losing his breath from his screams, he turns almost blue and starts grabbing for me with his little hands. Ellis's eyes are shut, and I don't know what to do. I shouldn't move Liam, but he's begging for me to take him.

I drop to my knees. "Ellis, Ellis! Wake up. Please wake up."

"What happened?" Christopher yells from the bottom of the stairs. I hear his footsteps next as he runs up toward us.

"Call 911, and tell them to send two ambulances!" I hold Liam still by the thigh and chest. "Momma's right here, sweetie. Don't move." *God, I want to pick him up.*

"Ellis. Can you hear me?" It's noisy now as Christopher stands next to me on the phone, and Irene is present, too, crying and asking what she can do. Ellis opens his eyes and tries to focus.

"Oh, thank God," I mumble.

"Is he OK?" he asks, referring to Liam.

"I don't know, but you both need to stay still in case something's broken."

"Cammy, the ambulances are on their way," Christopher announces from beside me. I look to Ellis, and he furrows his brow.

"I don't know if Liam hit the floor. I tried to prevent it."

"I know. I saw," I say. My head is spinning as Liam continues to scream over us. The sounds billow in the grand hall, and once I see blood seep out from under Ellis's head, I feel like I could faint.

I don't know how much time passes before I'm moved out of the way by Christopher so the paramedics can get through. He pulls me to his chest and rubs the back of my head.

"He'll be OK. He's crying, and that's a good thing."

"I only went to use the bathroom, and when I came out, he was already at the top of the stairs. I tried to get to him. I swear I tried," I say before I'm sobbing, too.

I pull away once the EMTs stabilize Liam's neck and get him strapped down on the backboard. I grab his hand as they lift him.

"Momma's right here. Everything's going to be OK." I look back at Ellis as he starts to stand. The EMTs yell for him to stay on his back. Grumbling something, he looks to me with an array of emotions. Confusion, anger ... fear.

Shit, Christopher.

I have no time to explain as paramedics start down the staircase with Liam. My son comes first, so I follow them to the ambulance.

CHAPTER TWENTY

Ellis

I fumble as I type another text to Camilla. We've been communicating back and forth since we arrived at the hospital hours ago.

One of my arms is in a sling, and I'm about to remove the damn thing and launch it across my room in the ER, along with my cell phone. Autocorrect is royally pissing me off.

She replies to let me know she and Liam are on their way to my room. I carefully lay my head back against the pillow. God, what if he'd been hurt or killed? All because of my fucking stairs—my wealth—my pretentious life.

And what the hell is going on between her and Christopher? I'm not surprised he hasn't shown his face. He's probably worried he'll end up in the ER next.

Camilla's head pokes inside before she steps in the room. Liam's latched on to her like a monkey, and she's holding his legs snug around her waist.

As she comes closer, I see that he's asleep. Once she spots the knot on my forehead, she frowns and gently touches the skin next to it.

"I'd lean over to kiss you if it wouldn't wake him."

"You're fine. Sit. We have things to talk about. Are they sure there's nothing more serious wrong with him?"

"Yes, they're sure. Did you not read the fifty texts I responded to with that same answer?"

"Do you not see how I still have one good hand?"

She gives me a wary smile. "He was examined thoroughly. He has a goose egg on the side of his head, along with a nasty bruise on his arm, but they don't believe he has a concussion. I'm supposed to keep a close eye on him tonight, just in case, but it could've been so much worse.

"As soon as he got a sucker and some cartoon bandages for his boo-boos, he was back to his old self. You saved him."

"No, my fucking stairs almost killed him."

She shakes her head. "No. He's my responsibility. I should've insisted on doing something about the stairs."

"The both of you are *my* responsibility, and you did tell me how you felt about the stairs when you moved in."

"Look, I could easily say this is my fault for leaving him alone or for yelling at him. He's had no trouble taking the stairs with us, so he probably fell from turning to see me. It was an accident."

"Where the hell was Emma?"

"She went home sick. I put Liam down for a nap, and I thought he was sleeping when I went to the bathroom. I guess he was looking for me." Sighing, she runs her fingers through his hair.

"I'm sorry," I say. "I'll find a gate wide enough to go in front of the staircase, or I'll have one custom-made if necessary."

She giggles. "That's going to have to be a mighty wide gate.

"Fine. We'll move into a smaller house, or I'll add on to the ground level."

"Stop, Ellis. Liam's OK. How are you feeling?"

"Eight stitches to the back of my head, bruises and this damn sprained arm. I'm pissed. I know how to fall from my martial arts training. I don't know what happened."

"Your focus was on protecting Liam. The way you held onto him ..." Her head shakes like she's trying to shake away the image of us tumbling down the stairs. "You were determined to save him, not thinking about yourself at all."

She tears up. "Anyway, thank you." Looking down at Liam, she continues to glide her fingers through his hair. "Um, Christopher and Irene left.

"I told them to go home, and Fletcher's in the waiting room. He said he wasn't leaving without us, so as soon as you're discharged, he'll drive us home."

"Speaking of Christopher... Why the fuck did he touch you and call you Cammy? Any other time I would've laid him out cold."

Leaning her head back against the wall, she struggles to look at me.

"This is the thing I needed to discuss with you last night. I swear I was going to tell you."

My hand fists. "Tell me what?"

"I knew him before I moved in with you."

"He told me he'd never met you before. So, did you meet him while you were dating Tony?"

"No. He lied to me, too."

"I don't understand." I bring my hand up. "Wait. First tell me there's nothing going on between the two of you."

"No, there's not, and I'm hurt you'd suggest it, especially after the time we've spent together."

I purse my lips. "Just explain, Camilla."

"After you told Christopher that you were moving me in, he was forced to confess to me a secret he'd been keeping. Tony had him befriend me while I was pregnant with Liam. Your brother knew all along that he had a son.

"Once I found out I was pregnant, I left Octavia and went to work at a restaurant where I waited tables. I didn't return to Octavia until Liam was six months old.

"Anyway, Christopher started coming into the restaurant almost daily, and we became friends. I was clueless that he had another motive.

"He claims Tony wanted nothing to do with Liam and was worried I'd come after his money. So, he paid Chris to keep an eye on me and find out what my intentions were.

"Once Christopher told him I wasn't a threat, he could've disappeared, but he said he had already developed romantic feelings for me. We grew closer, but I've never thought of him as more than a friend."

"You lied to me."

"No, I withheld the truth, and you should understand why. I was terrified over having to move in with you, and I had a child to protect.

"Chris and I agreed to keep it a secret so that I would have a friend in the house. At the time, I felt I needed someone, Ellis. Someone who would look out for Liam and me. Surely, you can get that. I didn't know you then."

"But you still should've told me before today."

"I know. I've wanted to, but things went from bad between us to all at once good, and I didn't want to screw it up." She exhales a long breath. "I swear I was going to tell you last night."

"Where the hell do we go from here? He's fucking fired for sure."

"Please, don't fire him. I agree it has to happen at some point, but first you need his help in finding out who poisoned Tony. Your brother confided in him, so Christopher may have known who Tony's enemies were.

"Besides, I need to put distance between him and Liam gradually. Liam's fond of Christopher, and he'll wonder why he vanished from his life."

I huff, wishing there was something I could punch.

"Why didn't you tell me Tony knew about Liam?" I ask.

"I was afraid if I told you, you would fire Christopher and still make me move in, or you'd be furious over the whole thing and take Liam from me."

As he rests against her in the chair, I feel like shit for threatening to separate them. Now that I've witnessed their bond, I know the pain it would've caused them, and I hate myself for instilling that fear in her.

"Christopher's in love with you. How am I supposed to accept him being in the house every day?"

"You do it by trusting me. I don't like him, and that's not going to change no matter what he says or does. I promise."

Camilla

"This says you have a concussion," I exclaim as I read the patient instructions sent home from the hospital.

"I feel fine." Ellis rolls his shoulder back, grimacing from his pain. Or maybe he's grimacing over his arm being in a sling. It's probably a little of both.

"You were trying not to tell me."

"Because you need to focus on Liam, not me. I'm a big boy."

"Boss plays with big-boy toys," Liam says excitedly as his eyes bounce between us in the kitchen. I fold my top lip over my bottom, attempting not to laugh.

"What's he talking about?"

"He was upset you didn't read to him last night, so I told him you were playing ... with your big-boy toys."

Ellis grins for the first time today, and that devilish gleam returns to his eyes.

"There were definitely toys involved, but there was something else more exciting and sexy to play with that I enjoyed more."

"No. Don't try to schmooze your way out of not telling me about your concussion, and speaking of *Boss*, would you care to explain how that nickname came about?"

"Oh, my arm's hurting. I think I should go to bed." Hunching over, he groans dramatically, feigning pain, but the grin gives him away.

"I should run and get your pain medication. This paper says they called it in to the drug store."

"No. I'm not taking something that could affect my thinking."

"Then, will you please take ibuprofen?"

"That I'll do."

Struck with a thought, I bite my lip.

"You can't be left alone tonight ... and neither can Liam."

"I'm well enough to sleep alone in my room."

"OK, but I have to check on you frequently."

He rolls his eyes. "Maybe I need to call my mother to come over and take care of me."

"Oh, my gosh. We should've called your parents. Will they be angry at me for not calling them from the hospital?"

"Camilla, I was joking; I'm barely injured."

"Momma, I'm tired," Liam says with a whine as he tugs on my jeans. Picking him up, I then groan from the weight of him.

"He shouldn't be in your bed tonight. He'll run with that and want to sleep in there every night."

"I'll sleep in his then. It's big enough."

"Momma are you gonna sleep with me?" Liam asks enthusiastically.

"Yes, and since Ellis has boo-boos, and needs to rest like the doctor said, I will read you a story tonight."

Leaning back in my arms, Liam sticks his hand in his front jeans pocket and pulls out a *Spiderman* bandage.

"Here, Boss. This will help your boo-boo." He holds out his bruised arm. "See, put it on like mine is."

Ellis takes it from him and smiles. "I think we should save this for you. You might need a new one to put on your arm tomorrow."

"I better get him to bed. It's been a long day."

Ellis's fingers graze my cheek. "Don't worry about me, and get some rest. I can tell you're tired, too."

"Yes, I am, and I started my period at the hospital, so that didn't help the situation."

Ellis reveals a fleeting look of irritation before he messes with Liam's hair.

"I'll see you in the morning, *Mikey*."

"Night, Boss." Without giving Ellis warning, Liam stretches over and wraps his arms around his neck. Ellis's eyes widen as he stares at me, and it takes him a second to hug Liam back. "Thank you for—for catching me on the stairs," my little guy adds.

Pain flickers in Ellis's gaze, but he quickly recovers.

"Of course, Liam. I wouldn't let anything bad happen to you."

"OK, I guess we'll head upstairs." Giving Ellis a kiss on the cheek, I leave him alone in the kitchen before I become more emotional and cry. I could've lost them both today, and I don't know how I would've recovered from that.

Ellis

For fuck's sake. "Camilla, go back to bed," I say after my bedroom door creaks open. Neither of us can sleep since she won't stop checking on me every thirty minutes.

"I'm sorry." Her voice is timid, and I think I see her biting her lip clear across the room from the hall light shining on her face.

"You don't have to be sorry. I'm perfectly fine, so go back to bed."

"But, what if you fall asleep and then you're not fine. You won't know."

"You can't stay up all night watching both of us."

"I thought I was going to *lose* both of you today. I've never been so scared in all my life. Not even when I gave birth to Liam alone."

Fuck. There's a tourniquet around my heart now, squeezing it tight.

"Go back to bed."

Without responding, she shuts my door, and I feel like an asshole. Sharing with someone is new for me, much like having a woman and child in my home, but I made the bed I'm lying in, and I shouldn't hold it against Camilla. She's all about the *feels*.

She's also not why I can't sleep. I've been lying here, worrying about Liam, too, and imagining the worst. I hope they did check him out well enough at the hospital.

Dammit. Kicking off my sheet, I sit at the side of the bed and pull on my pajama pants. I'm lightheaded in an instant, and my head is pounding, too.

I'm pissed at myself for losing my balance when I grabbed Liam. Maybe I made things worse. This *caring* shit is painful, and I'm recalling why I kept my emotions shut off for years.

Camilla

Lying next to Liam, I stroke his silky hair. If his breathing slows too much, I panic and touch him just so he'll stir a little to ease my concern.

Ellis hasn't been nice to me the times I've checked on him tonight, and I'm curious if he doesn't want me in his room. He's never shown it to me or mentioned me sleeping in there with him. I can't help but wonder about it since we've slept together in my room and in the bed in the guest house.

The door opens, so I sit up. "Ellis, are you OK?"

"Come on. We're all sleeping in your room." Climbing off the bed, I pick up Liam and follow Ellis down the hallway. Once we're in my room, Ellis pulls back the bedding with his good arm and points. "Put him in the middle." I do as he instructs and lay Liam down in the center of my king-size bed.

"You don't have to sleep in here. I promise not to wake you up again."

"I want us all together," he says as he joins Liam, getting in on the right side. I pad over to the left, and once I'm in, we face each other with Liam between us.

"Can I ask why you don't want me in your bed?"

I hear his heavy exhale. "I do, Camilla. I think about it often, but I want it to be just the two of us, and I want to be well when I finally get to fuck you there."

"Oh," I whisper.

"I probably fell today from you and Liam tilting my world on its axis."

"You're regretting us being here."

"No, but I'll tell you what I am feeling. I'm envious of Christopher for knowing you and my nephew better than I do. You and Liam feel safer with him, and it makes me fucking furious. I'm jealous that he wants you, and I have an overwhelming desire to hurt him for it.

"I'm angry that my brother let you struggle instead of taking care of you and Liam, and although he chose to be a worthless piece of shit, I feel guilty for being grateful that it's me who gets to be with you and his son and not him.

"Oh, and my damn head hurts from the fall, so can we finally go to sleep? I've had all the *feelings* I can take for one day."

"I'm falling in love with you."

"Fuck."

CHAPTER TWENTY-ONE

Ellis

Waking up from the sound of Liam's voice, I open my eyes in time to see the door shut behind him and Camilla. She's pissed at me, and I can't blame her.

She proclaimed she was falling in love with me last night, and I told her to go to sleep. It was not my finest moment. If she hadn't been so worried about me, she would've gotten up right then. Instead, she only called me a jackass before exhaustion knocked us out.

Rolling over, I groan from how achy and stiff my body feels. The back of my head is throbbing where my stitches are, and my arm fucking hurts, too.

Once I think of the conversations I need to have with Camilla, Christopher, and my cousin Greyson, I realize today's going to suck almost as much as yesterday.

I ease my battered body out of bed and walk to my bedroom to get my phone. After I send Christopher a text to meet me in my office at ten, I call Greyson.

"Hi, are you busy?" I ask.

"Driving to the office. I was going to call you when I got there. Something interesting happened with Tony's estate. I got a phone call inquiring about his will."

"From who?"

"His birth mother."

"You've got to be kidding me."

"No, and I went off on the bitch. I can't believe she thought Tony would leave her money after she basically sold him to your parents."

"She gave up her legal rights. She's not entitled to shit."

"Right. It's all going to you, and I told her she'd be wasting her time to try to change that."

"Actually, I was calling you in regard to my own will. I need to see you today if possible."

"I'm packed with appointments, but I could do dinner."

"Great, uh, I can't go out today. Could you come here instead? Say around six-thirty? I'll have Irene fix us something."

"Sounds good. I'll see you then."

Camilla

"Camilla, I'm so sorry," Emma exclaims. She's clutching the top of her purple t-shirt as she examines Liam's injuries in the dining room. He proudly shows her his bandages, and then with round eyes, he raises his hand.

"We fell way far down."

"Oh, I feel so bad."

"Emma, this isn't your fault, and I'm glad you're feeling better."

"I am. I think I got sick from the greasy pizza I had the night before, but if I'd only stayed, this wouldn't have happened. I bet Mr. Burke will fire me as soon as he sees me."

"No. He doesn't blame you, and often I wonder if things are supposed to happen a certain way." I try to hide my annoyance. "I know this whole event gave *me* some clarity.

"Why don't you and Liam take it easy today and hang out in the family room? He doesn't need to be jumping around, and he's probably too anxious to focus on learning, so you can watch movies instead."

"Sounds good."

Emma helps my kiddo down from his chair, and as they leave the room, Christopher walks in. He sits across from me with a cup of coffee in his hand.

"Did you tell him?" he asks.

"I did."

"Is he firing me?"

"He's not supposed to."

"I'm surprised." Taking a drink, he swipes a hand over his short hair that's a touch damp and barely brushed. His eyes are heavy this morning, and his blue shirt is wrinkled. I guess he got about as much sleep as the rest of us.

"I'm not promising anything. The man's moody, so who the hell knows what he'll do? I did put the focus on me and how I needed a friend coming into the house.

"He understood, but he's still angry you lied to him. You need to convince him that it's honesty from here on out. If not, he's going to give you the boot for sure."

"You seem pissed this morning."

"Yesterday was long and stressful. I didn't get much sleep, and I'm tired of trying to read Ellis." Standing abruptly, I grab my plate. "I don't want to discuss it. I have schoolwork to do. Good luck with moody Mr. Burke."

On that note, I leave and head to my office. I need to call Sasha again. I've texted and called her several times since arriving at the hospital yesterday, but I haven't reached her. It's worrying me.

Ellis

Christopher sets a fresh cup of coffee on my desk before he takes a seat across from me.

"Irene sent that up. I'm glad to see you're able to get around today."

"Thank you, but we don't need to exchange pleasantries. I'm going to get right to the point. Why did you lie to me? Why didn't you tell me Tony knew about Liam and that you were friends with Camilla? You had the opportunity when I announced I was moving her into my home."

"I needed this job, and I wasn't sure if you would keep me around after that admission. I was caught off guard, and I apologize. I guess I should've known it would come out eventually since Tony left his estate to Liam in his will."

"What? Tony didn't leave anything to Liam. He left his estate to me."

Christopher's mouth opens, and he squints his eyes.

"He told me he added him to his will," he says bitterly.

I shrug. "Maybe he wanted to appear better than the piece of shit father he truly was." Lacing my fingers behind my head, I lean back in my chair.

"Anyway, I'm not going to be self-righteous and pretend I'm perfect. I made some poor decisions where Camilla and Liam were concerned, but you lied to me.

"She gave me the impression you wanted to protect her, yet had you told me Tony knew about Liam, I wouldn't have had the grounds to put her through what I did. I hope you realize *you're* the one who caused her anguish."

His jaw ticks and body stiffens, but he can't intimidate me.

"I didn't know you were blackmailing her when this all began. Once she told me, we worried you might take Liam regardless, so we made the only choice we could. You know, she doesn't wish to be here. She's even pissed at you today."

Sitting back up, I clasp my hands on my desk and give him a cold stare.

"Here's the bottom line. Camilla isn't being held against her will. She's been told she can leave at any time, and she's choosing to stay, so obviously she isn't too upset with our arrangement.

"She's happy living here, *being* with me, and she wants me in Liam's life, so I'm going to say this once; back the hell off, stay out of our *relationship*, and stop chitchatting with her."

I may not have known Christopher was in love with Camilla, but I sure as hell knew he liked her. I have cameras I can view from my laptop, and I was about to install audio on the fuckers because of how often he was seen talking to her. I even witnessed it this morning, but it stops now.

"I understand," he says through gritted teeth.

"On to the next matter. This will be shocking news, but Tony was poisoned. Someone wanted him dead, so you're going to cooperate with me and the detectives to figure out who that was.

"He had enemies, and seeing how you worked for him and was his close friend, you should know who some of them were, so start racking your brain."

Camilla

I'm working on an assignment in my study when my phone rings. *Christopher*... I wonder what transpired this morning during his conversation with Ellis.

"Hello."

"You're sleeping with him," he says angrily. "Admit it."

"It's none of your business."

"I knew it! Why? What do you see in him that you don't see in me?"

"I can't explain it. I've been drawn to him since we first met, and attraction is not something people can control. Then, after I suspected he was a good person inside, I started developing feelings for him."

"You can't be with him, Cammy."

"I think it's time you stop calling me that, and you don't get a say in this. Did you forget how you betrayed me for years? You want to talk about Ellis being so evil, yet look what you kept from me? You used the situation with Tony and Liam to get close to me."

"But I did it because I cared about you and that sweet boy. Ellis has never been in a relationship, and he's almost thirty-five. Do you honestly think he's going to keep you around?

"He'll only use you until he's bored. Then, he'll toss you aside like Tony did, and Liam will be in the crossfire. Is that the kind of mother you want to be?"

"This conversation is over."

"Only for now, Cammy. One day soon, Ellis will reveal his true colors, and then you'll be throwing yourself in my arms like you did the first day you were here."

"And that was a mistake. I've never purposely misled you."

"Deep down you care for me. I think you're scared to admit it since we could have something real and lasting."

"I'm hanging up now, and you need to get your temper under control if you're going to be around Liam. You're acting like a jealous boyfriend."

"No, that role goes to Ellis Burke."

I huff at him and end the call as someone knocks on my door. I thought not having a job would give me more time to devote to college, but that has yet to be the case.

"Come in," I yell. Ellis ambles inside the room, looking broken today. Because of his injuries, a part of me has the urge to run and hug him, but another part of me that's angry at him for last night is overriding that urge. "What do you need?"

"We should talk."

"I don't think that's wise right now."

"I know you're pissed at me, so we're talking about it until you're not."

"You can make the decisions in the playroom, but I always have another person's wellbeing to consider when we're out of it, and that's Liam's, so you're not bossing me, *Boss*."

"I don't see how this has to do with Liam."

Sighing, I point to the yellow chairs near my bookcases.

"All right, we'll talk."

Ellis limps over and sits down. He's in jeans and a black polo shirt, and I'm betting he used his sprained arm to button his pants.

"I know I picked a terrible time for my confession last night, but your insensitive response was uncalled for. I didn't expect you to say it back, but at least acknowledging what I said would've been nice. It left me questioning everything between us."

"Look, I'm sorry. It was a hellish day, and I was exhausted and in pain."

"And that's why I said it was terrible timing, but the rant you delivered left me questioning if this is too much for you to handle: me, Liam, us moving in here, a relationship, and the worry of keeping us safe.

"Add that stress to your grief over losing Tony and finding out what happened to him, and I fear you could change your mind about all of this."

His lips purse, and he shakes his head.

"That's a bunch of shit."

"Ellis, I have to protect Liam's little heart. He hugged you last night and thinks the world of you already. I can't have him getting crushed if the day comes when we have to go back to our old life. You and I need to slow down so this doesn't become too overwhelming for either of us."

"Come here." His gaze projects aggravation and desire, but mostly dominance. I want him, and I wish I didn't. I haven't risked my own heart being broken in years, and it's never been on the line like it is now with Ellis. It's scaring the shit out of me.

Moving past the small table sitting between us, I stand in front of him. "Kneel."

I do it and stare at the floor. It's my last ditch effort to hang on to some control. His fingers slide beneath my chin and raise it.

"Look at me, and listen closely. I want you and Liam here. I have no intentions to end what's happening between us. I've never been the best with words, but I do show how I feel with actions.

"Aside from when this all began, my actions have proven the depth of my attraction to you and the genuine desire I have to provide for you and Liam.

"Do you know what I think? I think your confession last night surprised you more than it did me. So, with that said, my Rose, stop looking for a fucking excuse to bail."

Ever so slowly, he leans over, taunting me with a seductive gaze. His lips press to mine and linger before they brush along my cheek and then my ear. His tongue traces the shell of it, stirring up a shiver.

"I'll never let you go," he whispers, "and as soon as I feel better, I vow to fuck the doubt right out of you."

My eyes close and my knees wobble as his searing breath coats my neck. His tongue skims, curving down to the dip in my throat before a husky sound emerges from him and vibrates against my skin.

"I want inside you at this moment. What you do to me ... what I already feel for you ... can't be put into words, Camilla. Let me show you one day at a time."

"I've never been able to count on a single person in my life, Sir. No one."

"Then I'll be the first."

CHAPTER TWENTY-TWO

Ellis

"Ellis, what happened to you?" Greyson asks the second he strolls into the family room. He's early, and I'm guessing Irene let him in. I'm resting on the sofa with Camilla, looking like a weakling, while Liam plays in the floor.

"I failed at preventing Liam from falling down the stairs. We both took a tumble instead." Greyson's eyes are round, his mouth agape.

"Are you two OK?" His gaze darts to Liam.

"We'll be fine. Minor injuries." It takes me a minute, but I manage to stand up. "Let's go to the dining room."

"Are you joining us, Camilla?" he asks.

Giving him one of her glowing smiles, she stands, too.

"No, Liam and I already ate."

"OK, then. It was good seeing you again."

"Same here. You both have a nice dinner." As she turns to me, a crease forms across her forehead. "Um, I'm going to ask Beatrice to come over tonight so I can check on Sasha."

Turning my back to Greyson, I give her a pointed look.

"Why are you just now mentioning this?"

"It's not a big deal. I shouldn't be gone long."

"OK, but call Fletcher to drive you, and have one of the two security men at the front gate ride along, as well." Her nod is faint before she sits back down and picks up her phone.

I sense a need to say more, but feeling a cramp in my leg, I start to walk toward the door to work it out. Greyson follows me to the dining room, and right after we sit, Irene hurries in to serve us drinks.

"I shouldn't laugh, but there's humor in you falling and then asking me to come over about your will today. Did your life flash before your eyes?"

"Yes, but mostly I was thinking about Liam. To be honest, I've never felt fear like that. Thank God he wasn't hurt worse. He only has some bumps and bruises."

"I guess we do need to update your will. Did you consider doing the paternity test?"

"Yes, and I agree it's wise. How accurate will it be? Like what percentage are we talking about if, uh, say I come back as the father?"

He lets out a clipped laugh. "That you're 99.9% the baby daddy."

"You're a dick."

"I can't deny that I'm loving this."

Irene bustles in and sets down the salads we'll eat before she serves one of her specialty pasta dishes.

"Can I get you anything else, Mr. Burke?"

"No, thank you, Irene. This looks great."

She leaves the room, and I examine my salad.

"Just out of curiosity, how much percentage shows when siblings of the parent in question take a paternity test?"

"I don't understand what you mean."

"For example, say you had a kid but weren't available to take the test, could Lawrence take it to prove you're the father?"

"Yes, if my brother took the test, the DNA would match, but the results wouldn't show as high of a percentage."

"Hmm ... what if you and Lawrence were only half-siblings?"

Lifting up a fork full of salad, he eyes it.

"The same, but I believe it'd be even less percentage." He shoves the bite of food inside his mouth, so I start to take a bite myself, but then his fork drops against the table, creating a loud ding. "Holy shit. You're not Liam's father, are you? Tony is."

Damn, I didn't think I was that obvious. I recall what I said to Christopher about deceiving me and how I've already lied to Greyson once. I can't bring myself to do it again. Exhaling a weighted breath, I lay down my fork.

"OK, I'm sorry I lied. He's Tony's child."

Clearing his throat, my cousin wipes his mouth with his napkin.

"I—wow. I don't know what to say to that."

"It's complicated."

"You think?" He runs a hand over his blond hair. "Why did you tell me he was yours?"

"I want my parents to believe he is. You know how badly my mother wants me to marry and give her grandchildren. If she finds out Liam is Tony's, it will be yet another reminder that my brother wasn't hers. She'll be bitter at my father all over again for having a blood-related grandchild."

"As far as I remember, your mother always treated Tony like he was her flesh and blood. Are you sure this isn't about you?"

"What are you saying?"

"Are you really dating Camilla?"

"Yes."

"Then are you sure you're not worried what people will think when they find out the woman you're living with was once dating your brother? Or how the child you're raising is his?"

"That's absurd. I don't care what people think about me."

"Bullshit. We all care, whether we admit it or not."

I drag a hand over my mouth. "OK, fine. A part of me thinks this will stir up less gossip and drama if people believe he's mine. They won't have to know that Camilla ever met my brother. But it's mainly about my mother. She'll be ecstatic thinking Liam's her grandchild."

Greyson shakes his head. "Man, this is a twisted situation. I'm the attorney to your brother's estate, and now you just confessed that he has an heir. It's a big fucking deal, and don't you want him to have Tony's money?"

"Liam doesn't need his money. He has mine for now, and once he's an adult, I'll give him Tony's money through a trust. You can help me set that up."

"What about Camilla? Doesn't she want Tony's money to help raise her son? She has to wonder if you'll kick her to the curb at some point."

I glare at him. "I wouldn't do that. I'll take care of them no matter what the future holds. The only thing up in the air is what we'll tell Liam."

"Look, why don't you take the DNA test first. The results should come back fast. I think we need to determine he's definitely Tony's before we move forward. If by some off-chance he's not, you may not want to add him to your will."

"I know the test needs to happen, but this won't go over well with Camilla. She's going to think I don't believe her."

"Surely, she can appreciate the kind of wealth on the line. Hell, she might want Liam to have Tony's money, and maybe she can't find the courage to tell you."

"Right ... I hadn't thought of that. We'll get the test right away, and in the meantime, keep this news between us."

"My lips are sealed."

Camilla

"Thank you, Beatrice, for rushing over. I hate leaving Liam this soon after the accident, but I have to check on my sister."

"It's no trouble at all." Her grey hair is pinned up in a bun, and I stifle a giggle when I see her black orthopedic tennis shoes below her long black skirt. I pray I don't dress like that in my sixties.

"This is more than I should ask of you, but could you discreetly check on Ellis a time or two, as well?"

Giving a knowing smile, she nods. "Yes, ma'am."

"Thank you again. I'll try to hurry back." Grabbing my purse off the table near the door, I slip out quietly.

Greyson and Ellis have been talking a while, and I've worried Beatrice wouldn't get here in time for me to escape without an interrogation.

I didn't call Fletcher to take me. He lives nearby and is somehow at Ellis's beck and call. No, I have to do this alone, and my sir will be pissed later, but I'll deal with him then. He will want to punish me, and I'll happily oblige.

In my old car, I drive past the security guys and wave. One gives an anxious, puzzled look before he nods. Yep, I'm probably getting them in trouble, too.

I drive far across town from Ellis's, and it's like I'm in another world when I near my dilapidated, ugly brown apartment building.

The realization creates a sting of guilt in my chest for living here with Liam, but I remind myself that I was doing the best I could under the circumstances.

I park next to an old pickup that's in my assigned spot. I wasn't about to bring the new Mercedes here. It would be gone once I'm ready to leave.

As usual, music is blaring as I approach the door, and I guess I'll be lecturing Sasha. She's going to get us kicked out of this place if she keeps it up.

Once I unlock the door, I push it open, but it stops as the chain lock catches. In frustration and so she'll hear me over the music, I pound on the door. Rusty's face appears through the small opening where the chain is fastened.

"Well, well, well, look who came by to slum it."

"Cut the shit, and let me inside my apartment."

"I don't think so."

"Excuse me? I'm not playing, Rusty. Let me in."

"No. Go back to your mansion." He rubs on his dark goatee that matches the color of his stringy, long hair.

I grab my hip. "Where's Sasha? Get her now."

"No."

"Then I'll call the cops."

"You're bluffing. Your sister already blabbed that there's a reason you'd never get the cops involved, so you're going to go back to that rich asshole and pay the bills on this place every month so we can live here."

"The quota of blackmails I'll tolerate for the year has been met, so you can kiss my ass." I pull out my phone from my purse. "I'm calling the property manager. He'll kick every one of you out."

"See, I thought of that, too, but after he sees what's going on in here, he'll then call the cops, which puts us back to that whole issue again, and we already established how you don't want the police showing up."

All his words are flowing out in an annoying singsong, and I want to reach through this opening and strangle his windpipe. Shoving on the door, I scream for Sasha. Rusty gives a smug grin that reaches his glassy eyes.

"She's not in any shape to chat."

"What did you do to her? What did you give her?"

"Go home, Princess. Your kind isn't welcome here." He slams the door in my face, and I let out the loudest groan. That fucking asshole isn't getting away with this.

My sister must've failed to tell him the environment we were raised in. Liam's being safely cared for at the moment, so I can handle this old-school.

Once I'm in my car, I root through my purse and find the business card Bruce gave me my last night at Octavia. I punch the numbers into my phone.

"Hello, it's Bruce here."

"Bruce, it's Camilla ... from Octavia."

"Cannoli girl, how's it hanging?"

"Actually, not good. I need a favor."

"What's the problem?"

"Do you have a couple of friends who could help you clean out a house for me? As in, clean the lowlifes out of my old apartment for me? My sister's inside, and she's in trouble."

"I told you I got your back, girl, and I meant it. I don't have to be at work for a couple of hours. Where are you?"

I shake my head. "This is crazy. I can't ask this of you. What if you get in trouble?"

"That's not gonna happen. I have special ways of making people stay quiet."

"OK, but only if you're sure. Let me give you the address...."

I hang up with Bruce, and my phone rings while still in my hand. *Shit. Ellis.* He already knows I disobeyed. Pushing the answer button, I hold it up to my ear and scrunch my nose.

"Hello."

"Are you still at your apartment?" he asks, with anxiety as an undertone to his powerful voice.

"Yes, and I'll be home later."

"I'm on my way to get you."

"No, Ellis, please don't show up here. I don't want you to see my apartment."

He growls in my ear. "What's going on over there?"

"I have it under control."

"I swear on the goddamn playroom that you're being punished for this, young lady."

"Punish me all you want to, but please don't come here." It's quiet on the other end of the line. "Ellis? Are you there?" He hung up on me. That can't be good.

CHAPTER TWENTY-THREE

Camilla

My foot is tapping, and I'm tasting blood from my lip by the time a white SUV rolls up next to me. Burly Bruce gets out of the driver's side.

He's in jeans and a tight black t-shirt that hugs his massive biceps. Two men, almost as tall and muscular, get out and stroll up beside him. One is African American, like Bruce, and the other Caucasian.

"This is Rob and my brother, Bing. They love cleaning up messes. Lead the way." The men nod hello to me and look toward the apartment building. I start to walk up the sidewalk, so they follow behind me.

"Let us go inside first to get the situation under control, and then you can come in and find your sister."

"OK. I can't thank you enough for this. Rusty has long, dark hair. Just don't let my sister get hurt, and I really need this to happen without the cops showing up. I mean, I know you can't be super quiet—"

"I got this, Camilla," Bruce says, grabbing my shoulders. I suck in a noticeable breath and pull free to shove the key in the door. I unlock it and back out of their way.

Like the chain lock's made of paper, Bruce busts right through it with his friends storming in behind him. I hear his deep voice over the music, and then I hear Rusty's and another male's.

Next, there's yelling and the sound of some thuds and rumbles, maybe someone's back slamming against the wall. If the cops don't show, it will be a miracle. The only saving grace is the fact that most of my neighbors don't want them here any more than I do.

Sasha. Where is she in all of this? Knowing my sister is safe is all I can think about, so I step through the doorway. Bruce is putting a beating on Rusty, and his friends have laid out a couple of other guys I don't recognize.

There's a girl in only panties curled in a ball on the sofa, and she's crying. The music, fighting and yelling combined with the scent of drugs and filth is all too much for me.

My throat's closing up, and my sight blurs as fear consumes me. *No.* I have to get it together for Sasha. My eyes dart around, looking for her, but she's not in the family room, so I swing open my bedroom door.

My sister is sprawled out on the bed in a tank top and panties. There's a rubber band tied around her arm and a needle next to her. Running to her side, I rip off the rubber band. I clutch her shoulders and shake them.

"Sasha, wake up. Sasha." She opens her eyes, but they roll back in her head. Her mouth is hanging open with a film of drool at each corner. "Sis, can you hear me?"

"Yes," she mumbles.

"I'm taking you to the hospital."

"No." She tries to shake her head. "I'll be OK. I'm OK," she slurs.

"Then you're going home with me, and tomorrow I'm taking you to rehab." Realizing I can't pick her up, I stride toward the door to see if Bruce can carry her out. I come to an abrupt stop when I spot Greyson, Ellis, and one of his security guys.

With a puffed out chest, Ellis rips off his sling. The Velcro makes a loud noise over the music as he pulls it apart, and lord, could this night get any worse?

He's yelling at Bruce, with a finger in his face, as anger drips from his words. The security man and Greyson are toe to toe with Bruce's friends. Spotting me, Ellis exhales in relief. I run and slide between him and Bruce.

"He's my friend, Ellis. He came to help. I'll explain later, but right now I have to get Sasha home. She's in my bedroom."

The girl on the couch is still crying as she dresses. Bruce shuts off the stereo and begins talking to her. I follow Ellis and Greyson into my bedroom, and standing next to my bed, Ellis grumbles something under his breath.

"Can you carry her out for me?" he asks his cousin. After Greyson wraps my sister's exposed body in the blanket that's beneath her, we head back to the living room.

I approach Bruce and nod toward my sister's three so-called friends who are lying lifeless on the floor. Their scrawny asses didn't stand a chance against him and his friends, especially while high.

"Will they be OK?"

"They'll live, but they won't forget it. I told that Rusty he better never step foot near this place or your sister again. I

think he was about to cry, but I didn't give him the chance."
He brandishes a grin like this event was no big deal. "I'll tend
to this mess. You go."

"Thank you. I'll call you tomorrow, and I owe you dessert."

"Camilla!" Ellis shouts at me from the door. Bruce scowls
and points at him.

"Are you safe to leave with that guy?"

"Yes, I promise." Landing a kiss on his cheek, I scurry
toward the door. Ellis says something to the security guy
before the man strides toward an SUV.

Following Ellis and Greyson to an expensive car I don't
recognize, I then help Greyson put Sasha in the backseat. She
falls over, her body limp on its side.

Leaving her be, I walk around to the other door. With flared
nostrils and a locked jaw, Ellis holds it open for me.

"I'm sorry," I utter.

"Get in. Now." Lowering my gaze, I do as he says, lifting
Sasha up to make room for myself. The door slams shut, and I
jump.

Greyson starts up the car, and soon the silence is deafening,
seeming far more chaotic in my mind than the various loud
noises I heard inside the apartment. Greyson must feel it, too,
since he turns on the radio.

The ride across the city seems like an eternity. Sasha moans
on occasion, rolling her head from one side to the other, and I
keep saying a prayer she won't puke in a car that I would guess
costs a few hundred grand. Worrying she's cold, I pull the
blanket snugger around her.

This is humiliating. Greyson and Ellis saw my drugged sister in her panties and were in my apartment at its worst. Hell, they've probably never seen the inside of a place like that before.

I worry Ellis will struggle to forgive me for this. We can't go a day without issues, and it's quickly wearing on us. Even after what he said to me in my study, I can't help but feel like baggage he won't be able to handle.

It's why I tried to leave him out of this ordeal tonight. I needed someone to get rid of Rusty, and that's what Bruce and his friends did, but I betrayed Ellis. I really screwed things up.

Ellis

Greyson carries Sasha upstairs and to one of the spare bedrooms. For once it's good I have so many. For years this house was empty and quiet, and now it's like I'm running a damn hotel.

I'm guessing by now Beatrice is in another bedroom, watching over Liam from the monitor. I installed them in almost every room.

"Thank you, Greyson," Camilla says without looking him in the eye as they both cover her sister up in the queen-size bed.

"No problem." He's staring down at Sasha, scratching the back of his head. "I'm going to take off." He passes by me at the door. "Don't be too hard on them."

"Thanks for the help." Once he's left us alone, Camilla trudges over to me. Dropping to her knees, she takes hold of my hand with both of hers.

"I'm sorry I disobeyed you."

"*Sir*."

"I'm sorry I disobeyed you, Sir."

"We'll discuss it tomorrow."

"But I don't want you to be mad at me."

"I'm not mad; I'm fucking furious. Take care of your sister, and I'll check in on Liam."

Bowing her head, she nods and let's my hand slip from hers. I leave her alone, once again feeling as if a hundred different emotions are crowding my head and worming under my skin.

On one hand, I'm impressed as hell by what Camilla was brave enough to do to help her sister, but why didn't she let me be involved? I thought I made it clear that I'll be the one to protect her.

Granted, I'm not in the best physical shape to fight tonight, but I don't think that's why she hid from me what she had orchestrated.

Am I always going to feel this out of control caring about her and Liam? It's brutal, and I have this eerie sense the stress has only just begun.

***

A knock on my bedroom door wakes me, and it opens before I can respond.

"It's Camilla. Can I come in, Sir?" It would've been nice if she'd chosen to be this submissive *before* the stunt she pulled last tonight. I glance at my clock and see it's 4:00 a.m.

"Yes, you can come in." Rolling over to my back, I groan from the ache of my muscles stiffening back up. I have a feeling the second day of pain is going to be worse than the first. "What do you need?"

"Sasha is doing better and sleeping, so I had to come see you. I feel terrible about what happened." Her voice is coming from beside my bed, and I realize she's on her knees next to it.

"And I told you we'd discuss it tomorrow. I think the wait is a good punishment for you."

"Please, Sir. Let me make it right."

"Do you feel terrible about the decision you made to carry out this plan without me or terrible that I found out about it?"

"I didn't plan it. I only called Bruce after Rusty wouldn't let me inside to see Sasha."

"But you chose to call him instead of me."

"That night you gave me the terms in your car, you called me a washed-up dancer and said I had a strung-out sister crashing in my *atrocious* apartment. Once I got to my place tonight and saw how bad things were, I was ashamed.

"We grew up differently than you, Ellis, so I thought you'd be disgusted with me if you saw the inside of my apartment or how my sister was choosing to live. I knew it wouldn't have the same effect on Bruce after what he'd dealt with working at Octavia."

Dammit, how did this get turned around on me? I did say those things to her that night in the car. I made her out to be trash, but she's not.

I know the decent woman she is. I've witnessed the love she has for her son and those around her. She's not a part of the world I saw her in tonight.

"I understand why you would have that worry, but I told you only hours before you left that I wasn't letting you go, so you should've trusted me."

"I know, and I'm sorry, Sir."

"Get in this bed with me and sleep." I move over and make room for her. She climbs in, and the second her smooth legs and warm body are pressed against me, I want to roll on top of her, but it has to wait.

238

I'm not fucking her in my bed until I can give it to her for as long and as hard as I choose to.

CHAPTER TWENTY-FOUR

Camilla

After I've shown Sasha where everything is for a shower, I walk down to Ellis's office. From the doorway, I watch him rub his eyes, and I feel guilty. I'm well aware of the exhaustion he's dealing with after the last couple of nights.

"Hi, can I come in?"

"Of course."

"Sasha is showering, and Emma is doing schoolwork with Liam in the family room. I hope you don't mind, but I packed some of my clothes in a suitcase for Sasha. She doesn't have much at the apartment, and I don't feel it's safe to go over there today, anyhow."

"That's fine. We can send her more if we need."

"Send? I can take them to her at rehab."

"About that … shut my door, and sit down please." Taking a seat in front of his desk, I stare at him.

"You told me Sasha already spent time in rehab centers in our area, and it didn't help her for any length of time. I think we should try a different approach.

"Everything has been arranged for her to go to Passages in Malibu, California. She'll fly there later today for their inpatient program."

After his words, my mouth might be touching the floor.

"There is no way I can afford for her to stay somewhere like that, and I can't allow you to cover it."

"Allow?"

"What I mean is it wouldn't be right for you to pay. She's not your responsibility."

"This affects you and Liam, so it is my responsibility. I want her well so what happened last night doesn't happen again. You could lose her, Camilla, and I feel you've lost enough in your life. Besides, I'm not the one paying for her stay."

"If you're not, then who is?"

"Don't worry about that. All you have to do is get her on that plane. Fletcher will drive you both to the airport after lunch. Then, a driver will pick her up at the airport in California and take her to the facility.

"You can fly with her, if you prefer, but I didn't think you'd want to be away from Liam this soon after his fall."

"You're correct, but what if she refuses to go?"

"Don't let her. Help her see how this is a once-in-a-lifetime opportunity for someone in her financial situation. Show her their website and convince her this is for the best. Sasha will be gone a while, but she'll have a better chance at recovery."

Tears prick my tired eyes. Every time my sister has relapsed, this is the kind of treatment I've dreamed of being able to afford.

"I could never repay someone for this, and I could never express the gratitude I feel at this moment."

"Just because someone is wealthy doesn't mean they deserve treatment more than Sasha does."

Standing, I swipe the tears away from my cheeks.

"If you weren't aching everywhere, I'd sit on your lap and squeeze you hard with a hug. I'll show my appreciation soon enough." I do stroll around his desk and softly kiss his cheek. Reaching around to grab my ass, he smiles.

"I'll be ready to collect very soon."

***

While I drink coffee at the dinette set Christopher ordered for the kitchen, I study Sasha. She's eating toast across from me and hasn't looked up or spoken.

She didn't refuse rehab, but ever since I told her the news, shame has joined guilt on her thin, pale face, and they're on exhibit for all to see.

The doorbell rings, so I leave to answer it since Irene has gone to the laundry room. Opening the door, I find Greyson.

"Hi," he says.

"Good morning." I step back for him to enter. "I guess you're here to see Ellis."

"Yes, but I also wanted to check on your sister."

"That's sweet of you. She's much better this morning. Follow me, and I'll fix you a cup of coffee."

Coming to a stop, I spin around. "Oh, and I'll introduce you to Sasha, but please don't mention last night. She won't remember you, and she's dealing with enough shame this morning. She'd be so embarrassed to find out you carried her to the car."

Greyson smiles. "I promise not to say anything. I'm just glad she's accepting help."

"Yes, it's not easy for her—wait, how did you know about that?" My eyes round as I touch my fingers to my lips. "You're the one paying for her stay at Passages."

"You weren't supposed to know that." His brow furrows.

"Ellis didn't tell me. He only said it wasn't him, but you're the only other person it could be." I wrap my arms around his neck, forcing him to take a step back. "Thank you, Greyson. I don't know why you would do this, but I could never thank you enough."

"We all have our demons. I'm happy I could pay it forward for the support I received years ago." A throat clears as I pull away from Greyson. I turn around, and Ellis is eyeing us.

"Good morning. Camilla, can I have a word with you?"

I smile at Ellis's cousin one last time.

"Sasha's in the kitchen if you want to grab coffee and say hi to her."

"Thank you."

Once Ellis and I are alone in the hall, he rubs my shoulders.

"Is Greyson already trying to steal you away? The men in my family are known for pulling that stunt."

"No. I realized what he was doing for Sasha and had to thank him."

"He's a good guy under the arrogant, player façade he puts off. Listen, I need to drop another small bomb on you this morning."

"What is it?"

"We have an appointment this afternoon for a DNA test to prove that Liam is indeed Tony's child. Now, let me explain before you reply. I've never doubted that Liam is his, so don't think this is a matter of mistrust. It's only a legal formality.

"After talking with Greyson yesterday, I realized you could challenge Tony's will. You know I'm due to inherit his estate; however, Liam would be entitled to it if you prove he's Tony's son. You're smart. I imagine you've thought of that."

"I have, but he knew he had a child and still chose not to leave Liam anything. Tony wanted it to go to you, and I thought you'd be angry if I tried to take it away."

"I won't be, but I want you to know that regardless of your decision, I'm setting up a trust fund for Liam to one day have Tony's estate, and I'm also adding you and Liam to my will."

Ellis looks across the room. "In the meantime, it would mean everything to me if I were the only one providing for the two of you."

I touch his cheek, and he brings his gaze back to me.

"That's sweet, Ellis."

"I still want everyone to believe Liam's mine, but I'll respect your decision if you choose to challenge the will and say he's Tony's."

"I don't like talking about money or imagining how your parents would feel about this. If I say Liam is Tony's, then they'll think I'm after money from the both of you."

"They would see that's not true once they got to know you. Look, you don't have to decide today. Take your sister to the airport, and then we'll go take the DNA test.

"After that, I say we lounge for two days to recover from the last two." He smiles, and I notice he's still gripping my shoulders.

"You were supposed to put a new sling on your arm this morning."

"It feels better."

"I think you *want* it to feel better."

"That's true. It's sooner I can spank you with it." Tiptoeing, I press my lips to his.

"I can't believe I'm saying this, but I'm looking forward to it, Sir."

"Don't get him too excited," Greyson says. I take a glimpse at him, and he's grinning as he struts toward us. "He can't afford to wear out his one good arm."

"You would know about masturbating since you behave like a pubescent teen," Ellis quips.

I giggle. "Greyson, I would watch it. Ellis is sleep deprived."

"You must not know him then. He's cranky even with sleep."

Patting Ellis's chest, I smile up at him.

"I'll leave the two of you to your banter. We'll meet up later."

***

"Talk about something to take my mind off of this," Sasha says before she jerks her head back against the seat. I squeeze her hand as we ride in the back of the Mercedes to the airport.

"Did Greyson introduce himself to you?"

245

"Yes, and I can't believe you left me alone with that gorgeous man who's a million light years out of my league."

"I didn't intend to, but Ellis stopped me."

"Are all the Burkes that attractive?"

"All the ones I've met..."

"How old is he?"

"Thirty-one, I believe."

"It was awkward meeting Ellis before we left. He didn't flash me a grin like Greyson did, so I assumed he was angry with me."

"He's uncomfortable meeting new people. He's not mad at you, only worried."

Sasha shakes her head. "Unlike me, you fit inside their world. You're special, sis."

"I don't know about that. I'm worried all this will come to a screeching halt soon. I remembered more from the night Ellis and I were drugged." I look to her and scrunch my nose. "We had sex."

Sitting straight up, she turns to me.

"You two had sex that night, and you didn't remember?"

"Tony said he put GHB in our champagne bottle. You can have blackouts from that drug, especially when you're drinking heavily."

Sasha's hand smacks over her mouth, and her eyes bulge as she stares me down.

"Sis, did he wear a condom?"

"I don't remember, but I doubt it. I think it happened when we were close to passing out."

"Heelloo? Have you not pieced this together?"

"Pieced what together?"

"What if Ellis is the one who got you pregnant? I mean, that kid is the spitting image of him."

My eyes glance to the partition, and I'm praying it's soundproof. I can feel my lunch rising to my chest. I taste the bile next and swallow it.

"No." My head shakes as that one word races through my mind, over and over again. "No, no, no. It was one time, and I don't even know if he finished. I slept with Tony at least twice that week before the party."

"Have you forgotten the speech you love to give me about how it only takes one time to get pregnant?"

"This is different." I hold up my hand to count off my fingers. "Tony and I had sex regularly for two months before the party, I don't know if Ellis even came that night, and maybe he was actually wearing a condom."

I roll my eyes over my last comment. Ellis Burke has yet to wear a condom with me while sober. Regardless, I don't believe he got me pregnant. The odds are too slim, and the paternity test will prove it.

"It's not possible," I say to her again as I shake my head.

"OK. I'm sorry I mentioned it."

Pulling up at the airport, Fletcher retrieves Sasha's suitcase. I hug her ... touch her hair and brush her cheek. I feel like I'm sending my child away. She's sweating and pale.

"Please drink a lot of water on the plane, and make sure you eat something. Ellis put you in first class, so try to relax and rest, too."

"Yeah, I'm starting to feel it." She's hinting about withdraw, but neither of us wants to say it. "I'm scared," she mutters.

"I know, sweetie, but we can talk often, and I'll come visit. Do this for you, Sasha. You have so much life left to live."

Nodding, she squeezes her eyes shut to stop her tears, so I grab her hand.

"Come on. I'll go inside with you and help you get checked in."

"Thank you for giving me another chance."

"You deserve it. You're not our parents, and this place is going to help you see that."

CHAPTER TWENTY-FIVE

Ellis

Camilla's lounging next to Liam while I read him a bedtime story. The act of her fingers running through his hair has put him to sleep, so she quietly climbs off his bed and pads to the door with me.

After we returned from taking the DNA test this evening, Camilla sent Irene home and took it upon herself to order pizza.

She made chocolate chip cookies while we waited for the delivery, and then just the three of us had a quiet evening, relaxing in front of the television.

It was as if we'd been a family since Liam's birth. Camilla was comfortable, and he was, too, as he played on the floor nearby. The experience was foreign, yet I felt contentment for the first time in my life.

Even though I imagined I would settle down one day, I didn't believe there was a woman I could feel connected to, yet Camilla seems accepting of my odd personality, and she puts me at ease in my own skin.

As soon as we're in the hallway, Camilla smiles. Her hazel eyes gaze at me in an eager fashion as her hand slides up the front of my shirt and rests on my chest.

"Sir, can I have permission to do something for you?"

I smirk, curious where this is headed.

"Yes, you may."

"Good, come with me." Taking hold of my hand, she leads me to her bedroom. She grabs one of the handheld baby monitors off of her nightstand and pulls me to the bathroom. At the garden tub, she turns on the faucet and adjusts the water temperature.

Her smile afterward is shy, and her eyes struggle to meet mine. "Would you please let me bathe you ... among other things?" A woman has never asked me to take a bath with her, but I admit she had me at *among other things.*

"I'll agree as long as I direct you."

"Thank you, Sir." Her radiant grin and lift of her shoulders convey giddiness, and I suppress a chuckle over her eagerness to experience this.

Setting the monitor by the sink, so we'll hear Liam if he stirs, she then gathers towels and washcloths from the closet and lays them on a bench nearby.

"Strip down for me," I say. Her smile vanishes before she removes her sweater. She strips off the rest of her clothing, and her seductive gaze keeps me fastened to all the beauty she possesses.

As she stands naked before me, her long hair cascades over her shoulders, and the tips of the strands touch her pointed nipples.

My eyes peruse her curvy body that's speckled with light freckles, and the thought of no one knowing they're there, beneath her clothes every day, turns me on more. She's mine, and her creamy skin and beauty marks are only for my eyes to see.

"You're so damn beautiful."

"Thank you, Sir." Her gaze drops, so I clutch the back of her hair and pull it downward, leaving her no choice but to look at me.

"Feel good about your body, Camilla. It's perfect in my eyes." Capturing her lips, I thrust my tongue in her mouth. As she kisses me back, she moans, and the needy sound thickens my dick on the spot.

Her desperation is evident from the pressure of her fervent tongue. It strokes over mine before she sucks it in like she can't get enough.

Remembering the water is running, I pull back and glance at the tub. Almost full. "Undress me now."

Her eyes, hazy with desire, guide her hands as she unbuttons my shirt and pushes it over my shoulders. She works swiftly at getting my pants unfastened next, and eager like her, I help at removing everything below the waist.

I hold her hand as she steps down inside the large tub, and a faint purr leaves her swollen lips once her breasts dip below the warm water.

I can still see the rounded shape of them, and something about it makes my dick ache. I want to taste her wet nipples and caress her tits. Climbing in after her, I move to the end opposite the faucet.

"Sir, can I wash you?" Feeling self-conscious, she lowers her gaze, but I'm pleased she's making the effort to submit to me, pushing past her comfort zone.

"Yes, you may." She floats my way, so I open my thighs, letting her move between them. Sitting back on her legs, she begins washing my body with the cloth, starting at my chest and then moving to my good arm. The other one still aches like a bitch, but I won't dare tell her.

Her touch is relaxing but in an arousing sort of way, and I have the urge to touch her, too, so I reach between her arms to massage her tits.

Her nipples stiffen until they're so damn pointy and hard beneath my fingers. Needing so much more from her, I swipe the washcloth from her hand.

"Grip my cock. Stroke it—slowly." Dragging her teeth over her bottom lip, her fingers wrap around my shaft and begin moving up and down.

Slick, wet, and firm with pressure... It feels remarkable, and I may have to indulge in future baths with her. Stretching my arms out over the edge of the tub, I lay my head back and close my eyes. She strokes my dick, and I feel the buildup in my balls. She touches them, too, a tease to egg me on.

"Don't stop." Moving over my thighs, she straddles me, and I can tell she's trying to be gentle about it. She's worrying too much about my injuries, and she needs to stop that shit because I'm about to take her hard in this tub.

It might be my new favorite place. Of course, I haven't fucked her in my shower yet to compare the two. Oh, the things I look forward to doing with her...

Her hand releases me, and before I can lift my head, she sinks onto my cock. *Fuck.* I grab her waist and squeeze.

"You disobeyed and didn't ask permission first. That earns you a punishment."

She unveils a wicked smile, and it's one that exudes the naughty side she's growing more comfortable in sharing with me.

"Exactly," she coos. Clenching her hips, I pull downward, burying my cock so deep in her pussy that she cries out and digs her nails in my shoulders. She lifts up and sinks down again, and I groan from how incredible she feels sheathed around me.

We both move her up and down until I erupt. My head tucks and eyes snap shut as my orgasm ricochets pleasure throughout my body. Once I've soaked up every ounce of ecstasy, I open my eyes and stare at her.

"I think I'll let you off the hook for that one." Reaching down between us, I find her clit and rub languid circles. She whimpers, and her eyelids fall. "Touch your tits for me. Play with them, and get me hard again."

"Yes, Sir." She fondles her breasts before she tugs on her pink nipples and twists them between her delicate fingertips.

Growling from the sight of her, I apply more pressure to her swollen clit and rub her pussy faster. Already, my dick's waking up again as she grinds against it.

"Baby, I could never get my fill of watching you touch yourself."

"Sir, I'm going to come. Please, may I?"

"Yes." Reaching the threshold, she clutches the back of my hair, and a heady moan rushes from her cherry-stained lips. "Come, my Rose. Come for me now."

Camilla

After a couple of earth-shattering orgasms, my head rests on Ellis's shoulder. The water in the tub is cool, but neither of us want to get out. As his fingers run through my hair, he leaves tender kisses across my collarbone.

"I haven't done this before—taken a bath with a woman. I'm now a huge fan."

I giggle. "I must say I like it, too. Uh, have you had many women in the playroom?"

"Only you." His reply sends me upright.

"But you seem experienced at it."

"I've done some basic bondage play with women in the past, but that's it. I've fantasized for years about delving deeper into BDSM and having a playroom, but it had to be with the right woman and one woman only. I knew once we met it had to be you."

"I'm glad I'm the only one. I want to try more things and be all that you need. I owe you so much for what you've given Liam, me and even Sasha."

His eyes fall to my lips. His fingertips skim over them next before they continue along my jawline. He tucks a piece of my hair behind my ear, the act tender and intimate, and I tilt my head to the side to allow more of his faint touch. His fingers drift down my neck and on to my chest.

"Mmm..." I utter.

Swallowing, he presses his hand over my heart. He's deep in thought, and what he's doing isn't seductive. Instead, it's as if he's cherishing my body. Hugging me, he presses his lips to my hair.

"Don't ever leave. I need to hear you say that you won't."

"I'm not going anywhere, Ellis, and I pray you'll always want me here."

Pulling back, he cradles my face. "This is only our beginning."

One Weeks Later

Ellis

While Camilla is at a doctor's appointment for her back, I'm busy catching up on work. Emma's in the library conducting preschool with Liam, and Christopher is running errands for me.

The upstairs is quiet, and that's needed as I develop new malware to help with the FBI's ongoing battle against Tor-based child porn sites.

Until I square away my current contracts, I have to fit in more office hours. I was a workaholic before Camilla and Liam moved in, and time with them has shown me there's more to life than work, but I have assignments I can't simply walk away from.

My cell phone rings, so I groan until I see it's Greyson.

"Hey, man," I say.

"Did the DNA results come back yet?"

"I haven't looked today. I'm too damn busy, and I haven't been that concerned about it. Camilla isn't lying." I pull up my email account. "Let me check to shut you up.... Here it is."

"Open the damn thing."

Clicking on it, I scroll through the paragraphs.

"What the fuck?"

My phone beeps, signaling another call, so I pull it down and look at the screen. It's my security detail.

"Greyson, I'll have to call you back."

"Wait, what did the results say?"

Not replying, I switch to the other call and hit the print button on the email in front of me.

Too much shit is going on.

"Mr. Burke, this is Mitch at the front gate. There's a Rusty Jones here to see you. Would you like us to let him through?"

Rusty... Sasha's boyfriend. In the event he ever contacted her again, I took the time to learn all there was to know about the piece of shit.

"Ask him why he's here."

"Sir, he said he wants to talk to you about Camilla Rose." Bringing up the cameras on my laptop, I see an old pickup at the front gate.

"Tell him he can come up if he allows you to search him first."

Mitch puts me on hold, and I wait impatiently until he tells me that Rusty's unarmed and will be going through the gate. I march downstairs to answer the door.

Why does he wish to discuss Camilla instead of Sasha? That's what I'm eager to hear. I walk outside, and after the door of his truck screeches shut, he strolls up the walkway.

He stops about six feet in front of me, and I see the evidence of the beating he took a week ago: a faded ring of black around his eye, a red mark over his crooked nose, and blue bruises on his forehead and sunken cheek.

"I'm Rusty, Sasha's boyfriend."

"You mean *ex*-boyfriend."

"Maybe. It depends if you give me what I want." After taking a long drag off his cigarette, he flicks the ashes toward my lawn.

Gradually exhaling the smoke, his dark brown eyes squint and roam over my home and estate. "Damn, *Trust Fund*, you got a nice pad here."

"I actually have *work* to do, asshole, so what is it you're wanting?" While he continues to size up my wealth, I examine his torn jeans, dirty white t-shirt, and bare feet in loafers, which give him a homeless appearance.

His unkept hair is pulled back in a ponytail. He's overly thin, and his arms are decorated in tattoos, but if they weren't, I'm sure track marks would be visible. This man looks like nothing more than a penniless criminal.

"Tell me what you want?" I close in the distance between us. He's not stepping foot inside my home.

"Sasha's a talker while under the influence. She hinted about some dark secret from her past. I don't have all the pieces to the puzzle, but her sister, Camilla, is hiding something big."

"Their affairs are none of your goddamn business."

As a sudden rush of disdain colors his face, he points at me with the hand holding his cigarette.

"Listen here, motherfucker. I didn't press charges against those goons who showed up at the apartment last week, so you're gonna hear me out. If you don't give me cash, I'll figure out what it is those bitches are hiding and make an anonymous call to the cops."

"You're fucking with the wrong man. I know everything about you and your pathetic existence, including your rap sheet. I don't see how you have the upper hand here. If you don't want the cops knowing where you hide out, I'd leave now."

"I'm already getting sent up. I just need cash for an attorney to help me get a lesser sentence. I have nothing to lose by telling the cops about Camilla.

"I know you're good for it. Just give me the damn money, and I'll never breathe near Sasha again. I was about done with her slutty ass, anyhow. If you don't help me out, I'll sic my friends on Camilla the way she unleashed hers on me."

Displaying a sinister smile, he takes another drag from his cigarette. "*And*, I'll find Sasha when I get out of jail. Maybe I'll make it my life's mission to meddle in yours. Oh, and to discover Camilla and Sasha's dirty secret."

I pierce him with a dead stare. "How much are you wanting?"

"Ten grand."

Jesus christ, the heroin must've fried his brain cells if he thinks that's all the cash I'm good for. Hell, I'm a little insulted he's not asking for more.

"Fine, but if I give you this, you better never show your damn face here again, and don't even think about blackmailing me a second time. I have connections that would put you away for the rest of your life."

He smirks. "You got it, weasely man."

"Stay right here," I sneer. Leaving him alone on the walkway, I head inside and lock the door behind me. I march to my office, and after counting out some petty cash, I put it in an envelope and head back downstairs.

Along with refusing to give him the money, I could make him pay for this stunt, but my gut tells me he'll turn up again at some point, causing us trouble.

I want Camilla to feel safe. She's already watching her back at every turn because of her past, and I'm working on easing that burden for her. If this will help, it's worth every cent.

With a heavy exhale, I hand over the money. "Now, get the fuck off my property." He flips through the envelope with a smug smile on his mauled face.

"Sure thing. It was nice doin' business with you." He strolls away and flicks his cigarette across my manicured lawn. Reaching his truck, he turns back and rubs his goatee. "I still think that bitch of yours should have to pay for what she did to me, so for that, I'll tell you a secret."

"And I told you to fucking leave." I take the few steps back to my front door and open it.

"You think you only recently met that girlfriend of yours, but that's a lie."

My hand freezes on the door knob before I turn back to him.

"What the hell did you say?"

To be continued...

END NOTES

Thank you for reading *The Terms: Part One*. *The Terms: Part Two* releases June 2017 at Amazon, iTunes, Barnes and Noble and Kobo.

Keep up with release information at www.rubyrowe.com. You can also follow Ruby on Amazon, Goodreads, Facebook, Twitter, Instagram, Pinterest, and BookBub.

If you enjoy Ruby Rowe's writing, you may like romance stories under her other pen name, Scarlet Wolfe.

Lastly, if you enjoy my writing, I'd greatly appreciate it if you would leave me ratings or reviews. Thank you!

ACKNOWLEDGEMENTS

Thank you to my amazing husband, Patrick, who didn't hesitate to support my desire to write under an additional pen name.

Like always, he wanted to support my dream, even if it added more work to my hectic schedule. I am so blessed to have such a patient man by my side.

Family and friends, I love you, and I appreciate you lending me an ear to blab to about my books.

Readers, thank you for taking a chance on *The Terms*. I couldn't write full-time if it weren't for passionate book lovers like yourselves! I feel blessed anytime someone reads a story of mine. I hope you'll check out all the future releases by Ruby Rowe.

Rosa Sharon, my PA, thank you for helping promote my first full-length novel. I believe your knowledge, experience and efficiency will add so much to my success. I look forward to us becoming good friends.

Samantha Wiley, I can never thank you enough for all you do. You're a great editor and a wonderful friend. I'm happy "Ruby Rowe" gives me another excuse to talk with you every day.

If you need editing or proofreading, Samantha and Rachel can help you at Proofreading by the Page!

I want to give a big shout out to Jo-Anna at Just Write. Creations for creating the sexy cover. She always produces fantastic work!

Alfie Gabriel is the handsome man on the cover. Alfie, I'm grateful to present you on the cover as the hero of my novel, Ellis Burke.

Pink Ink Designs, thank you for the amazing photograph!

Thank you to my beta readers, Jennifer Balmer, Dana Gallie, Morgan Mittelbrun, Rachel Pugh, Karina Wade, and Samantha Wiley. Your feedback is invaluable.

Bloggers, authors and readers who are sharing *The Terms* with your followers, I'm so appreciative. You have busy work schedules and personal lives, yet you use a portion of your precious time to help me succeed.

I can't thank you enough. Thank you, as well, for leaving reviews. Good or bad, they're important for both readers and authors.

Happy Reading!
Ruby

CPSIA information can be obtained
at www.ICGtesting.com
Printed in the USA
LVOW07s1547070617

537271LV00010B/687/P